ISAAC CAMPION

" 'Yer glad our Dan's dead! Tha's glad Daniel's dead, just so's tha can blame Laceys!' I yelled at him.

"Me father's fist sent me reeling against the door-jamb. I should never have said it. It was a terrible thing to say to a man who'd just lost his favourite son. But that's what I shouted."

Daniel's death at eighteen is a terrible blow to the whole Campion family. His parents lose their favourite son, Isaac and little Becca lose an adored elder brother and their father loses an excellent horseman and dealer to carry on the family business. At first it seems that the more timid Isaac is trapped forever in a life he hates and can only watch as his father's bitterness and violence against the Laceys grows.

ABOUT THE AUTHOR

After a childhood spent in East Anglia and Cumbria, Janni Howker had a strong sense of coming 'home' when she settled in Lancaster, less than twenty miles from the cotton mill where her grandfather and great-grandfather went to work when they were twelve. She studied at Lancaster University and did several jobs: working with elderly and mentally handicapped people, and as an assistant on an archaeological site.

Her books are acclaimed world-wide and have won prizes in Britain, Holland and America. Her *Badger on the Barge*, a collection of stories focusing on encounters betweeen young and old, is also a New Windmill. *Isaac Campion* won her the Somerset Maugham Award, a travelling scholarship awarded to a writer under 35. It had never before been given to a writer of a children's book.

ISAAC CAMPION

CAMPION

JANNI HOWKER

HEINEMANN
NEW WINDMILLS

Heinemann Educational Books Ltd
Halley Court, Jordan Hill, Oxford OX2 8EJ
OXFORD   LONDON   EDINBURGH
MADRID   ATHENS   BOLOGNA
MELBOURNE   SYDNEY   AUCKLAND
IBADAN   NAIROBI   GABORONE   HARARE
KINGSTON   PORTSMOUTH (NH)   SINGAPORE

ISBN 0 435 12326 2
1004650556

Copyright © Janni Howker 1980
First published by Julia Macrae Books 1986
First published in the New Windmill Series 1988

91 92 93 94 95 13 12 11 10 9 8 7 6 5 4

Cover illustration by Anthony Browne

Printed in England by Clays Ltd, St Ives plc

October 17th 1984

Dear Miss Howker,

I read in the newspaper about your first book, so I am sending my congratulations. It said in the newspaper it was about young folks and old folks. Here is a notion for you! I am 96! My legs are no good any more and my chest is bad but I have still got my brains in my head for which I am thankful, though it is all a damn nuisance and I don't reckon I'll see another winter out.

I was born in Hardacre in 1888. It was all horses at that time of day and no tarmac on the roads like now. My father was a horsedealer and a rough sort of man I must say, though my mother was very respectable. There was another dealer lived half a mile away. They called him Clem Lacey. My father and him hated each other like cats hate dogs. It was not just a bit of rivalry. It was what you might say was unholy hate. I have a notion folks had stronger feelings in them days when there was no telly to keep them quiet. I have often puzzled over how that hate began and I am not much nearer the reason now than I was then. But it is what it did to my brother Daniel in 1901 that I am wanting to tell you. That's when this business I'm trying to tell you began . . .

Don't cry,
hit him in the eye,
hang him from a lamp post
and leave him there to die.

[Children's playground chant]

ISAAC CAMPION

AN ACCOUNT

Chapter One

Now THEN, I was twelve, rising thirteen, when our Daniel got killed. Aye . . . it was a long time ago. I'm talking about a time of day eighty-three years back. Eighty-three years. It's a time of day that's past your imagining. I'm talking about a different world. You might as well say it was a different planet, the world I was born in.

No radios. No televisions. No World Wars. They'd not even built the *Titanic*, let alone sunk her. This is it, you see. This is what I'm trying to tell you. When you look back over all those years, you think that what happened was bound to happen. You can't imagine that it could happen any different.

They've got this notion about the past, about history – they forget that folks lived in it – well, we didn't know what was going to happen. It's the same for the young ones, they think they are going to live forever. And good luck to them, I say! Good luck to the young ones, let them live to ninety-six! Let them live to a hundred!

Eighty-three years back . . . It's me that should be dead and buried in my grave, but I'm telling you, I can remember the day Dan died just as clear as *that*!

There's me and Joe Flitch, the clogger's son, crouched in this muddy little drainage ditch behind the schoolhouse on Chapel Street. Stinker Beck, we called it. Crouched in the smelly yellow mud, we were, where no one could see us.

1

"Go on," I says to Joe. "Go on. I dare thee! Eat one!" I was egging him on, you see.

We'd been let out of the school-room after a day of chanting times-tables and "Twelve inches make a foot. Three feet make a yard . . ." with tall Miss White-head glaring down at us like the eye of God! She was a terror, was that schoolmistress. We were all scared of her.

But she couldn't see us in the ditch. "Go on!" I says to Joe. Just to see if he would. Poor Mazey Joe starts sniggling and snorting. He wasn't right in the head. He wasn't the full shilling. We were always daring him to do daft things. The pleasure wasn't in teasing him. Teasing Joe Flitch was too easy. No. I'd say the pleasure was in thinking up something crackers enough for him to do so's you could tell tales about it afterwards.

"Ah can, Isaac! Ah can eat 'em!" he kept spluttering. "Ah swallered a clog nail once."

I can just see him – crouched in the mud like a fledgeling that's fallen out of a nest, with his tuft of hair bristling on his head, and his thin elbows and knees poking out of his clothes. Spitting and giggling.

I was watching the water dripping between his fingers, and these two tadpoles were wriggling and stranded in his hand. Well, I didn't really believe that even Mazey Joe Flitch was daft enough to eat a tadpole.

I should have known better.

"Oh, put 'em back," I says. It was giving me knee-ache, squatting there, and anyway I wanted to go and meet our Daniel outside *The Bear and Staff*. So I was just going to reach out and knock the tadpoles off his hand and back into the ditch, when Joe suddenly stops giggling, claps his hand to his mouth and sucks!

"Bloody goomer!" I jumped up, yelling at him to spit them out. Well, it made me feel sick to my belly. Oh, it was my fault for daring him to do it, but that didn't stop me

2

feeling sick at the sight. "Yer goomer! Spit 'em out! They'll grow into frogs inside thee and tha'll die!"

Aye! That's how we talked at each other in them days – right harsh. Right broad speech, as you might say. I couldn't have understood a man from London, and he'd not have understood me.

Any road, Joe Flitch was as simple as a smack on the head, and he just laughs and says, "Ah can eat ants an' all, Isaac!" That's what he says! "Ah can eat ants an' all!" And he's grinning all over his thin little face . . .

Eighty-odd years ago . . . And there's me scrambling out of the ditch, feeling sick to me guts. But that afternoon was only beginning. April 17th 1901 . . . That was the day of our Dan's death . . . That day's fixed in my mind like a picture. Do you know something? I can even smell that day . . .

This is the only way we have, you see, to go back into the past. This business of remembering. But it is false. You can't go back because you know what is going to happen. But you didn't know what was going to happen then, you see? You did not know. You are just living your life, wondering what it is all about. You don't know what might be important. You don't know anything.

And that's how it was. There's me, off like a shot, scrambling over the school-yard wall and jumping down into the cobbled street. It was all cobbles then, or setts, and that's a bad surface for running on. I could hear Mazey Joe clattering after us in his heavy clogs, with his skinny legs going like a pair of scissors, but I didn't want him near me. Oh no. Not bloody likely! Not after he'd done that. Well, I shot round the corner of Chapel Street and nearly bolted a hitch of dray horses outside *The Turk's Head*. But when I looked back to see if he was catching up, Joe had stopped to watch the fellers rolling the beer barrels off the cart and into the cellar. They used to make a lovely soft thundery sound, those wooden casks, when they were rolled across cobbles.

And I didn't stop until I'd put a safe distance between us,

then I hawked up in the gutter. I kept thinking, what if them tadpoles really are still alive inside him? Swimming about in his belly! I can remember Dan telling me once about some feller at a fair in Ireland who ate live chickens and killed rats with his teeth. But tadpoles! That's the trouble. You don't believe owt until you've seen it with your own eyes.

Mind, I wasn't what you'd call squeamish. In them days you couldn't afford to be. They'd a different notion about things then. And I'd seen pigs killed. Pig-sticker comes. A lot o' shrieking. Collect the blood in a bucket for your black-puddings. Scrape off the bristles in scalding water. Often. Often, I'd seen that. Or me mother would ring the neck of a hen. Or I'd a knacker's nag to take down to Harry Black's slaughteryard. Of course, I'm not saying it's any different these days, is it? If you want to eat bacon, you've to kill a pig! Only it's all "get someone else to do the dirty work" now. Hide it from the children! It's hidden from everyone.

Any road, all I'm saying is, that it turned my stomach, them tadpoles. I suppose because it was my own fault.

But I soon perked up. Did I tell you it was April? And I was on my way to meet Dan. So I took a short-cut through the old rope-walks to the river. You know where they built that big comprehensive school? River View? That used to be the old rope-walks. An April day – sun scudding out between grey clouds. A primrose sun, my mother would have called it, and clouds hung up like washing. But the lanes and alleys were all a churn of muddy cinders and cart ruts, and on the streets the cobbles shone like grease . . . Aye, it was one of them clear, cloudy April days when you can hear the whistle of a train and the clanking of wagons being shunted in the goods-yard from right across the river. And I'll tell you a funny thing. They still used horses in the goods-yard and in the shunting of wagons then. But my father would never sell a horse to the railways. He never did, and he never would. I don't know why.

And here's another thing. You're the first person I've ever

4

told about Joe Flitch eating those tadpoles. I was going to tell Dan, but I never got the chance. It's like I've been ashamed of it for all these years – ashamed of having made him do a cruel gormless thing like that. He did it to please me – poor half-baked little beggar . . .

I'm saying that now, but I began to see the funny side then. There's me walking along with me hands shoved in me pockets, frowning happily, thinking that perhaps we could send Mazey Joe to me Uncle Howard in Doncaster. Set him up in a booth alongside me Uncle Howard's fairground boxing-tent. We could charge folk a penny to watch Joe eat tadpoles and fart frogs! Joe Flitch – The Human Heron! Perhaps I could have trained Joe to eat sticklebacks an' all! Or maybe clog-nails, horseshoe-nails, spoons! The Human Ostrich!

I could just imagine us travelling round the country, going to all the fairs. To Skipton, Barnard Castle, Macclesfield, Durham and Brough. I would say it was a better idea than Joe Flitch ending up in the County Asylum like he did do. Oh, but I was always one for great notions. Always trying to think up schemes so's I wouldn't have to spend the rest of my life in my father's stableyard on Oven House Road.

Well, I come out of the rope-walks onto River Street, just by the vicarage there, just as the clock of Saint Michael and All Angels strikes four, so I thought I'd better get a move on, or else Dan would have shifted from *The Bear*. But I was out of luck! The vicar was in his garden, standing by his rhubarb patch, frowning like a soldier along the length of a rake.

Watch theesel' here, lad, I thought. And I tried to sneak past quietly.

You see, the Reverend Armistead always collared me if he saw me, as if it were somehow my fault that me father and Daniel never went to church. This made my family different from all our neighbours. Religion was the big thing, and it made you respectable. My father had been beaten with the

5

rod of religion by my grandfather, until all he wanted was to break that rod over his knee. We were not respectable, though it is hard to admit it. And my father resented this bitterly, but he had cut off his nose to spite his face. He would not go to church. He would not go to the same church as Clem Lacey. With me mother – well, that was different.

So I'm trying to go invisible, creeping along under the lilac trees by the vicarage wall. I just knew that if I didn't get to *The Bear* soon, Daniel would have gone off for a few jars with some of the other dealers' sons who'd come in for the auction. Truth is, I was only guessing that he'd still be at *The Bear* because they held the auction in the yard behind it. And I was sure my brother would have had to stay to the end, because we had horses for sale in all four classes.

Usually, my father would have been there and all, but I knew he'd be up at the tramways' stables on Coulton Street, because he was sorting out a big deal he'd made with Bill Grafton, the stables' manager.

I didn't want nabbing by the vicar when there was a chance of a sup of Dan's beer! A chance of sitting outside *The Bear* when me father wasn't about! I always felt, you see . . . I always felt I could act older when me father wasn't about. Somehow, when he was watching me, everything I turned my hand to, I made a mess of. I could tie a good strong knot if I was working alongside Daniel, but if me father saw, he'd yell, "Yer bloody gormless nowt! Do it o'er!" And that bit of rope would just fray into tangles in my hands! I couldn't do anything right for him.

Oh aye, things were bad between me and my father long before Daniel died. But I didn't know how bad they were until after me brother was buried.

Well, I thought I'd got past the vicar, when I hear,

"I say! Young Campion! A word! I say, boy!"

It didn't do me any good, pretending to be stone deaf, because he was as quick as an adder to his garden gate.

I had to take my hands out of my pockets. My mother

would have clipped me if she'd seen me standing with my hands in my pockets in front of the vicar. Perhaps me father would've laughed. I don't know. I can't ever remember making my father laugh.

"Well," says vicar.

And I said nowt. I wasn't going to give him any help at all!

"And how is Mrs Campion, Isaac? I couldn't help but notice she was missing from the church on Sunday. Is she well? How is your mother?"

"Middling," I says. I was damn sure I was going to make it hard work for him. How can I explain? In those days, your *real* neighbours knew all about your mother. They knew about everything. They didn't ask questions – they told yer! 'Yer mam's been ill, then,' or, 'That's a grand new top coat yer father's wearing. Got it ordered special from Alston's, didn't he?' So you just felt that when the vicar, or someone, asked such-like questions they were strangers. And difficult strangers to boot. Because they had power, and somehow you felt they knew more about you than they were saying.

"But is she ill? Is Mrs Campion ill, Isaac?" he says.

"No."

"Oh, I see. She wasn't in church last Sunday. She's not ill then?"

"No, I told yer." Oh, I could play that game for hours. I wanted to get away to *The Bear and Staff*, but I was stuck. And the vicar's frowning, and he starts jabbing the handle of his rake at a slug which was crossing the garden path. I'll tell you, it made me feel like spitting again, seeing that slug knocked to one side, curling up like a tadpole. Reverend Armistead went on jab-jabbing at it, missing, and rapping the paving stones. Getting right worked up, he is!

Well, he gives me that smile. Changing tack. A sort of smile you get off superior people and that you're supposed to feel grateful for. Here's the vicar of Saint Michael's smiling at the son of rough Samuel Campion, the godless horse-dealer on Oven House Road. Oh, right benevolent!

7

I didn't smile back.

"Well then. So your mother is in good health. And your father? Mr Campion? Is he well?"

Now this was a fickle question. He was just trying to spy on my father through me. "Aye, " I said. You see what a stubborn rough beggar I was?

"Good, good. He'll be in Ireland, will he not?"

"No."

"Oh? I thought he'd have sailed for Ireland by now. Doesn't he usually go in the Spring? To bring back the horses? I was sure he would be in Ireland."

Me, I was watching that slug uncurl, poke its feelers out and sneak off towards the primroses at the side of the path. I was sweating cobs for it! Wanting it to get away, just to spite vicar! Mind, I knew I'd have to say something to him, or he'd have kept me there till next Preston Guild.

"Me father doesn't stop her coming," I says. "Becca was sick, Sunday last."

The trouble with that man was, give him an inch and he was after the full furlong. The slug might have made a clean getaway under the primrose leaves, but I was still stuck there, and the vicar started going on about my father and about Clem Lacey. Now Clem Lacey was this other horsedealer, and the man my father hated. And the vicar's saying he can't understand why two men should fall out with each other, just because they're in the same line of trade.

Now I'll tell you something. I'll tell yer summat for nowt – and ask any lad and they'll tell yer the same! When a stranger starts talking to a lad about his father, that stranger is treading on thin ice. On black ice. Whether it's blame or praise he's saying, that stranger should not be talking to a lad about his father! If it's praise he's saying, you feel you're falling foul of his comparisons, so to say. And if it's blame he's saying, well, you nettle up. You bristle all over! Well, that's how it was for me. I was having

8

enough trouble getting me father straight in me own head, without the vicar putting his ha'porth in!

So when he starts saying, "Mr Lacey at least manages to put his feelings aside on Sundays. As did Mrs Lacey when she was alive. I often see him in the same congregation as your mother." That was too much for me.

I was twisting right up. Raging at the vicar, standing so superior there at his gate between the lilac trees. And it just comes spitting out. "Only reason Clem Lacey goes to church is for fact tha bought horse and trap off him," I says. "And he gets cut o' weddings and funerals wi' hiring off his black mares and that hitch o' dappled greys! He'd not come else! Me father'll not bend his knees to thee!"

There's me, twelve, no taller than that man's garden rake, but that's what I said. Then I ran off.

"Isaac! Isaac!" vicar shouts. Shocked. But I was already away over Kingdom Bridge.

Perhaps I shouldn't have said it. But on balance, I reckon still that it was Reverend Armistead's fault for winding me up.

And I'll say this one thing in favour of my father. He wasn't a hypocrite like some of our neighbours – sin all week and say a prayer on Sunday.

And he didn't comment on religion. He didn't care if a man was a Baptist or a Catholic or a Radicalist, as long as his coin was good money. The only prejudice I ever heard from his lips was one night when he'd been out drinking and he'd come back full of beer. "It's like Hell in *The Black Swan*," he said, "you can't see the fire for Methodists."

Well, two things had happened since I'd got out of the school-room – and they say things happen in threes. Perhaps my life would have been different if I'd thought that then and gone home. Aye, that's what they say – things happen in threes. But I'm not superstitious though my father was a harshly superstitious man. Me, I say things happen, and if you can remember three things that happened on the same day, you're doing well.

No I'm not superstitious. I'd walk under a ladder on Friday the thirteenth, and then kick the first black cat that crossed my path, just for good measure! You've enough to face in life, without keeping one weather-eye out for shadows.

But if that vicar had only kept me talking for a while longer. If he'd only done that . . . I'd not have seen what I seen. I'd not have remembered this day. Who's to say? I'd have grown into a different man. I'd not be telling you this now.

So there's me, running off across Kingdom Bridge and on the other side of the river it was all the tall black warehouses of Kingdom Quay, then the town rising up the hillside behind, like it does to this day. I was dodging between horses and carts, heading up onto the main street, still running, with me bootlaces whipping me ankles. It was leather bootlaces then. And whip! By Christ! They'd leave great welts on yer ankles if they smacked your bare leg when they were wet!

And I was full of anger and full of shame. Shame at what I'd yelled at the vicar and fear of me mother getting to hear what I'd said. And anger because the vicar had kept me talking and I was sure I'd have missed me chance of finding Daniel and having a sup of his beer. But the worse thing was this – the vicar had stirred up in me all that hornet's nest of fears I had about my father.

You see, the only person I'd ever talked to about this looming bad feeling between me and my father was Joe Flitch. Daft Joe Flitch! And then only the once. Summer before, I think it was. Me and Mazey Joe swinging on this branch of an elm tree overhanging the river. I remember Joe says, "Ah wish I were thee, Isaac. Ah could gallop horses! Ah can! I'd not be frit o' galloping!"

"Tha'd be frit o' me father, Joe," I says. On this branch,

10

we were, bouncing lower and lower, with our heels almost splashing in the river.

"Aye," Joe says. Serious. Not like Joe to be serious, you see. "Aye," says Joe. "Aye, I would an' all. I'd forgotten tha father . . ."

But I'd not said owt to anyone else. And there was the vicar, stirring it all up!

Well, that's how it was. It was nowt unusual for me to be running along wishing I wasn't me. Wishing I could be someone else's son.

Well, I got up into town and someone shouted at me across the street. It was one of our neighbours waving from his cart. "Eh Isaac! I've just seen thee father!"

"Where?"

"Up Coulton Street – outside tramways, talking wi' Mr Grafton. Them's masterpieces, them horses he's sold to tramways."

"Have yer seen me brother Daniel?"

"Aye. Were yer looking for him? He's up at *The Bear*, and you can tell him from me that I don't like that moustache he's sportin' – makes him look like a right little highwayman! Like a right little Dicky Turpin!"

Well *that* was a neighbour talking, not a vicar. You get my meaning now? And it cheered me up. It was a bit of luck. Dan was still at *The Bear*, so I ran off into Market Street, but I'd soon to slow down again. The street was full of traffic – dog-carts, traps, landaus, old blue wagons of farmers. Aye, it was jam-packed with the farmers and stock-breeders and dealers who were leaving the auction yard behind the pub. Private buyers, and all. And a constable in a black cape was keeping an eye on the strings of horses being led down the street.

Stick yer elbows out, put yer head down and charge yer way through that lot!

Oh, it's a different time of the world I'm talking about. Going up the street with the auction spilling out – well, it

11

was very exciting to me. I could smell beer and horses. Smell the sweat of fast bidding and money on the men's clothes. All jostling and arguing. All these farmers and bargemen and dealers come in from miles around. It was a great gathering. All these men, all wanting to talk – they'd maybe not seen anyone but their wives and neighbours for the whole winter. You could smell it on them. The auction was over, and now it was all devil-may-care, arguments, a belly full of beer and a bit of scrapping to round the day off!

And there's me trying to swim against the tide, so to say. Them all coming down the street and me trying to wade up it. You got jostled and knocked and damn near trampled under foot!

"Sorry, lad," some feller says. Then he goes on quarrelling with his mate. "I'm telling thee, that chap was a buyer from the war office!"

"Was he nowt!" says his mate.

"Why do yer think dealers were shoving prices up? Of course he bloody was! Buying up remounts for the army in South Africa. I'm telling thee, Jack. You'll not be told nowt!"

When I saw them all, all those buyers and dealers, I wanted to be in with it. I wanted to be like my father and like Daniel. In the pit of my belly, it excited me. But when I was alone in our stableyard with my father – well, I didn't want owt to do with horses at all.

All that rough crowd – it was like a bazaar to me. The hard black hats and the top hats, the soft caps, mufflers, different voices. Yorkshire men, Irish, East Lancashire, perhaps a man from up Durham, a couple of dealers from Westmorland . . . Aye, men from all these foreign parts were bulging past you on the street, and it filled you with wonder that there could be so many different ways o' speaking in this world! It was always the same for me when I was a boy. When a buyer came into my father's yard, it wasn't the deal, the cash, I was interested in. It was the man. A different life

12

from a different place . . . Over the hills and far away, that's where I wanted to be, from the moment I was born.

Any road up, there was Daniel at last, sprawled on a bench behind the fancy iron railings in front of *The Bear*, not caring that his long legs are stretched out fit to trip folk over. And he's looking round, trying to see who's yelling his name among all that great throng. It were me, of course! But I was on the other side of the street and strings of horses kept blocking me view.

Now then, I'd just got clear of a couple of grey mares, and was crossing over, when I saw that someone else was standing in the doorway of *The Bear*. And this was Dick Lacey, Clem Lacey's eldest lad. He would be sixteen. Because Dan was eighteen when he got killed, and Dick Lacey was somewhere between me and Dan in age. A tall skinny lad, with his cap shoved right back on his head, and a bit of beer inside him, I dare say.

Well, I was glad my father wasn't about – not with one of the Lacey lads being there, or there might have been some unpleasantness. He never missed a chance to have a go at a Lacey, didn't me father. He was as unbending in his hatreds as he was in his views about religion. If he took against a man, he told him to his face what other folks would only say behind his back.

Well, I went and parked myself on Dan's bench. And he says, "What's tha' come here for? Yer not having any o' me beer, so yer needn't bloody well ask!"

That's how it is sometimes with brothers. I'd break a leg chasing after Dan! I'd think it a royal privilege to be in his company! But when you're eighteen, you don't want a twelve-year-old hanging onto your shirt tails.

"Oh, go on, Dan," I says. "Let us have a drop."

"Go on then, yer beggar," he says.

So I had a swig of his beer. And that had made my day. Just to be sitting beside Daniel outside *The Bear*, watching this street full of people . . .

13

And now I'm telling you this – now I'm having to think about these things deeply to tell you this – I think this was the way of it. Because me and my father couldn't see eye to eye, I'd made a second father out of our Daniel. In my heart, I mean. Can you understand that? He stood between me and my father's harshness time after time . . .

But then it comes. I'd just started telling Dan about Mazey Joe, when Dick Lacey must have seen us. And out of the blue, he calls to Dan.

"Tuppence, Campion! Tuppence, tha' can't jump yon rail!"

Daniel looked round, a bit surprised. He hadn't seen Dick Lacey there until then. Then he said, laughing, you know, "Yer like throwing yer money about, Dick Lacey!"

But, "Sixpence!" says Dick Lacey. And he meant this fancy railing between the pub and the street. And that's how it went. This business between our two fathers. It was Laceys trying to make fools out of Campions, and Campions trying to make fools out of Laceys, in front of everybody.

"Sixpence!" Dan shook his head. He didn't believe Dick Lacey had that kind of money. But he handed me his beer and got up off the bench. Well, I was proud he'd taken the dare. I wanted him to show Dick Lacey up. So he ran and thrust his hands between the spikes of the railings, flipped his long legs clear over the top, landed like a cat – and slipped.

This wrought iron fleur-de-lis barb had pierced his armpit and gone into his ribs. But Dan was laughing! Like he'd just banged himself. Just winded himself! I stood up cheering, because he'd won the bet. Then Daniel wasn't laughing. He was gasping, and there's blood squirting over his shirt. That's when we saw he was stuck like a pig. Impaled on a spike.

Men came running across the street, swarming out of *The Bear*, some of them half-drunk, all trying to rescue Dan.

They lifted him off, but they tugged him a bit and all his shirt was sloppy with blood. And he kept crying out.

Me, I was still clutching his beer, and I was still carrying it when I followed after the cart they laid Daniel on. It was a farmer's cart and they laid him on some sacks.

A man was sent running to fetch the doctor, but that man met us as we were crossing Kingdom Bridge. The doctor was out with the midwife.

"Then get to vetinary then!" someone yelled, but another man says, "There's not much use, mate. By the look on the lad, it's too late for that. Poor beggar."

Aye . . . That's how me brother died. April 17th 1901. And I shall never forget looking through the slats of the cart. The side of his face, and the way his lips were stretched back over his teeth . . . I was a grown lad of twelve, but one of those men picked me up in his arms and carried me home. And that is the truth of it.

Chapter Two

IT HAD TO BE DICK LACEY, didn't it. It could have been any mortal else – but, no, it had to be Dick Lacey who dared our Daniel to jump . . . Anyone else, and my father would have seen my brother's death for what it was. A cruel accident. Just two half-grown lads larking about. Showing off. But my father'd not see it that way. From the moment those men carried our Dan into the kitchen and laid him out on the table, he talked of nothing else but the Laceys. He started raging in on the subject even as my mother was taking off Dan's shirt and washing the blood off his poor dead body, and he was still raging on that subject three weeks after Dan's funeral. It was as if revenge mattered more to him than grieving, and when he sent for my uncles three weeks after the funeral – well, we knew it could only get worse.

Me, I did my fair share of sobbing. I'm not ashamed to admit it. Seeing my brother laid out, all white and wan, in our parlour. Candles round the coffin. Oh, death was quite an event in those days. All the neighbours coming in to pay their last respects, and even the children nipped into the house to get one of the funeral biscuits my mother baked. They had a different way with death then. It was a big event then. Even my sister Becca could remember being held over the coffin to kiss Dan, though she wasn't turned three when he died.

The front curtains of the house were closed and we were dressed in black mourning. And I think that this was a good thing. Nowadays you might meet a young lad on the street and you'd not be able to tell that his brother had died recently – not from his clothes, nor from his mother's clothes. All you've got to go on these days is the grief in the eye. So I think that this business of making a big event of death was good. Everyone could see that something sad had happened and they'd treat you accordingly. Everyone could see you were grieving and so nobody was pretending that everything was normal, you follow me? Because life in a family is not routine when the eldest son dies, or when any of that family die. The way people are about death these days, you'd think they'd die just from talking about it! Brr! Don't mention that word – we don't want to hear that word! No one ever died from talking about death.

Then comes the funeral. Oh, I wept until I'd wept myself dry. The black plumed horses. The black streamers floating from the drivers' tall hats. Dan's coffin being lowered down into the earth ... My brother's funeral was the biggest spectacle the churchyard had seen since the death of Mrs Lacey. My father made sure of that. He went deep in his purse for Dan's funeral and he ordered a whole Garden of Eden to be placed on Dan's grave – vacant chairs of red roses, broken hearts of silk carnations, all sorts of fancy wreaths. He made a great show of it, but I can remember my mother stepping forward and she put a small bunch of primroses among them. She had picked the primroses herself out of our paddock and there were crumbs of yellow pollen on her black gloves. She gave my father a sad look and put her own flowers on her own son's grave.

And I went to the mason's yard with my father. I was there when he ordered the headstone. There were stones, uncut headstones, propped against the wall but in one corner of the yard there was a draped urn carved out of marble. "Right," says my father to the mason. "I like that one. How much is it?" So the mason mentioned a price. "I'll take it," says my father, "but I want it on a higher plinth."

"That will cost you a fair bit more," says the mason. "How tall do you want it, Sam?"

"I want it to stand two hands higher than the weeping angel on Mrs Lacey's grave," says my father. Aye, that's what he said, and this is how he was going on.

Well, as I was telling you, three weeks after the funeral my father sent for my uncles. At that time of the year he would usually have been in Ireland buying up horses, but he'd not gone. He'd sent some hired men instead.

On the day my uncles came, I was in tears again – and not because of Dan. But because my father had belted me. Aye. The afternoon Uncle Jack Campion and Uncle Harry turned up, I was hiding in the end stable, and I can remember that I was upset and I was clinging onto an old mare for comfort. Knotting me hands in her mane and hiding me bruised face in her neck and sobbing.

The far end of that stable had collapsed into tall nettles. My father never kept good animals in there. It was a dark peaceful place with only a few shafts of sunlight getting in through the cracked gable wall. And I stayed with that mare even after I'd stopped crying. I didn't want to go back into the house where my father and my uncles were talking. All that talk of the Laceys – I was in mortal terror of what they might be planning. I'd say that I really believed they were planning a murder, and I didn't want owt to do with it.

I can remember saying to this mare, "It's nowt to thee if it's a Campion or a Lacey as takes thee to the knacker's. Either road, tha's nobbut bully-beef for the army when Harry Black's hacked off thee head and hoofs . . ."

It gave me a cruel sort of comfort, you see, speaking to this old animal like that. The mare meant nowt to me. My father had taken her off some farmer's hands that morning. The idea was that he'd take her up to Harry Black's slaughteryard

18

on Tanner's Row, and he'd come out of the deal a few bob better off. He'd get a few shillings for the carcase.

There was an old wooden partition which separated this tumble-down end of the stable from the good end which my father still used. And through the planks I could hear the sounds of my uncles' horses moving about in their stalls. Have you ever stood in a quiet stable? They're calm under-watery sounds you hear. Shod hoofs scraping on the flag-stones. Soft spluddery thumps of dung. Deep-chested gentlemanly snorts . . . I can hear all those sounds now. I'd been used to those sounds since I was a baby. Since the day my father carried me in as a baby. "Is tha scared of girt horses, tha little devil?" he says, because I was crying in his rough hands.

Our Dan hadn't cried. "Our Dan damn near jumped out o' me hands onto t' back of a black mare – and he were nobbut two hours old!" My father often boasted about that.

Any road, I'd been hiding in the stable nearly all after-noon, with my head still ringing from my father's blow, but I'd watched my uncles arrive. I'd seen them through the crack in the wall. Uncle Jack come riding into the yard in a high wheeled trap. A hard black hat on his head, and he still had the same grim look on his face as he'd had on the day of Dan's funeral – only then he had been stone cold sober. My mother had been very strict about that. She would not have any drinking going on after the funeral. She made them all drink tea. She was afraid there might be trouble if the men got drink inside them.

But when Uncle Jack climbed down from the trap, there was a brandy flask in his coat pocket.

Then I spied on Uncle Harry arriving. He'd come all the way from Liverpool, and he drove into the yard in a hired dog-cart, with his gold watch-chain swinging across his waistcoat. I liked my Uncle Harry. He was in leather exports, not horses. After the funeral I'd heard him tell my mother that he was going to emigrate to America at the end

19

of the summer. He'd bought some shares in a canning business. Aye, Uncle Harry ... I'll tell you some more about him after, because he became a very important man to me in the next few weeks. But, do you know, he had the softest palms of any man I'd ever shaken hands with then, apart from the vicar. Shaking hands with him was like shaking hands with quality. Oh, I was very proud of my uncle's hands when I was a lad. But his knuckles – they were as hard as rivets.

So I watched him follow my father into the house. Two fighting uncles. My father's brothers. They'd helped carry Dan's coffin three weeks before.

And there's me, hiding in the stables, afraid of what it meant, them coming to the house again. But there was one more uncle to arrive. He didn't come till the following morning. My mother's brother, Uncle Howard Brank, from Doncaster. He hadn't come over for the funeral, and I hadn't seen him for at least four years. But by Christ! He was the uncle who scared me most. I did not want him to come to our house. I thought there would be trouble once he came. I thought there might be murder done. The thing was this – Uncle Howard Brank was a retired prize-fighter. And the picture I had of him in me mind was of four years previous. Flat nose. Scarred face. My mother had taken me to the fairground in Doncaster when I was seven or eight, and I can still remember the way my Uncle Howard cheered daft farm lads to their splattery doom in his boxing ring!

Oh aye. I remembered him as a big, laughing, vicious man. He'd made me – a little lad of seven – punch him hard on his bare belly. It was like punching a plank o' wood! And he made me keep punching until me fist was sore. Then he took me into this other little booth behind the main tent, and he fetched out this small wooden box and he made me hold it. Do you know what was in it? No, well, I'll tell you! A tarantula spider! A hairy great tarantula spider! "One bite and you're a gonner!" says me Uncle Howard.

Oh aye, he was a right character! He made a small fortune by betting grown men a week's wages that they couldn't hold a spider while he counted up to ten. When they'd taken the bet, he'd tip this great rearing eight-legged tarantula out of its box into their innocent palms! That's true! That's God's honest truth I'm telling you!

He lost that tarantula in the end, in O'Neal's – a bar in Liverpool near the docks. A Negro challenged it to a fight with a scorpion which *he* kept in a box. Scorpion stings the spider to death among the whisky glasses on the bar, and this black sailor wins five guineas off me Uncle Howard.

Aye, there were some characters in those days!

But you can see why I was afraid that something might happen once Uncle Howard turned up.

This was it. This was the thing, you see. If Dan hadn't have been dead I would have been glad my uncles had come to the house. I'd have hidden myself on the window seat in the parlour just so's I could listen to the stories they told. Stories as big as legends about all the things they'd done. But Dan was dead. And I'd got to thinking that me father and me uncles weren't bothered about him. I thought they were just glad of an excuse for a scrap with the Laceys! Any excuse for a barney! Oh, the whole of Oven House Road was buzzing with talk about what might happen, and it was like fat flies crawling all over Dan's corpse. That's what it felt like to me, and it made me feel sick to my belly.

That's why my father had belted me. I feared him like fire, but that morning he must have said something – I can't remember what – and I turned on him. "Yer glad our Dan's dead! Tha's glad Daniel's dead, just so's tha can blame Laceys!" I yelled at him.

Me father's fist sent me reeling against the door-jamb. I should never have said it. It was a terrible thing to say to a man who'd just lost his favourite son. But that's what I shouted. And then I'd hidden away in the stables, not just because I was afraid he might thump me again, and not

21

just because I was shamed to me very soul. Though I was. But because I wanted to thump him back! After he'd walloped me, I fair ached with wanting to clout him back, but I didn't dare to. Him, a great strapping man, and me, a twelve-year-old lad. Besides, it was a terror in me to find I should want to hit me own father . . .

Well, I couldn't stay in the stable hiding for ever, and it was getting dark outside. There'd be footsteps beyond the partition, and a bit of lamplight shining through the knot-holes in the planks. And that was Dick-William seeing to my uncles' horses. Dick-William was my father's stable-man. He worked for my father and he was paid forty-seven guineas a year plus luck-money on the sale of a horse. My father always dealt in guineas, never in pounds.

Well, I didn't want Dick-William to find me. He'd only ask about the bruises on me face, so I stayed very quiet until I heard him go away. You know, crouched there by that sick mare, until I was sure he was on his way to *The Turk's Head* with his terrier at his heels. Sometimes I liked his company. I used to sit on the corn-bins when he'd finished work some evenings, and listen to him and Dan talking dogs, rat-hunting. They were both beggars for the dogs. And I'd listen and watch them sharing a pipe, sprawled on the corn-bins in the lamplight. And that is a pleasant memory I have of being a boy – sitting on the corn-bins next to me brother, of a fine summer's night, and seeing the stars over the half-stable door . . . But that had come to an end now. Me brother was dead.

And now it was dark outside. And I had to go in.

"Isaac? Isaac? Where are yer?" That was my mother calling from the kitchen door.

I can remember I'd come out into the yard, and I was watching the shadows of my father and my uncles through the lace curtains which covered the bottom half of the parlour window. There'd be my Uncle Harry stooping to the hearth for a spill to light his cigar, and the tip of his cigar glowing red as he drew on it. Then my mother went into the room and closed the curtains, and the yard went black. The stars of the Plough were winking over the chimney pots, and the clock of Saint Michael's was chiming across the town. And this is how it had got, you see. I was full of a great loneliness, and feared to go into my own father's house.

"Isaac? Isaac?"

"I'm coming," I says.

Now I've not told you about my mother. She was called Alice. Alice Campion was my mother's name. But at the time I'm talking on, the trouble was this – since our Becca had been born, and she was two when Dan died, and then Lizzy, the new baby, had been born, there'd come a gap between my mother and me. Not a bloody great chasm, like between me and my father, you understand. No, this was natural. With these two little infants on her hands, she was too busy to be bothered with a big twelve-year-old like me, unless it was for fetching and carrying, or nagging.

That's why I spent so much time trailing about after our Daniel. There was a big gap of years between me and my brother and between me and my sisters, and this was because my mother had miscarried three children. They had died in her womb, and she miscarried them.

But I'll tell you something. Sometimes when I was alone with my mother, when Becca and the baby were asleep of an afternoon, say, I felt as though I was missing her even though she was in the same room as me. It was like part of her had gone away . . . She must have had a hard life, my mother. I often think what a hard life she had.

When our Becca was born, two years previous, I'd come across me mother sometimes with the baby at her breast, and she'd smile. A very quiet soft smile. But now, with this new baby, she hid herself away. I was growing up, you see. I didn't dare roam the house in case I came upon her with

23

her blouse unbuttoned. I felt it was my fault in some mysterious sort of way!

Aye, I was growing up, and this time when the baby was swelling under her apron, I'd guessed what she and me father had done to make it. Oh, no one talked about sex in them days. Name o' God, no! They kept you in the dark! But I'd learned that much from Dan and Dick-William's talk. It's daft, but I felt as if somehow me mother had seen into my thoughts like the eye of God and seen what I knew! It made me feel red with shame. But this is something I like – I like the way a baby's mouth will suck your finger as hard as a plug-hole if it gets the chance.

Well, as I was telling you, I went into the kitchen with her, and she lifts the lamp from the table. "Your father said he'd to clout thee," she says, holding this lamp to my face. She'd still be dressed in black mourning, and there'd be a lock of Dan's hair in the brooch at her throat. "He said you were gone to skulk in the stables. Stay still! Let me look!"

Well, she was dazzling me with this lamp thrust under me chin. She wasn't really being rough with me – it was just that she'd had enough to put up with without me and my father fighting.

"God alive! Look at the state of yer!"

"It's nowt," I says.

"I could clout thee meself. Look at state! Where's them clean hippins?" And she fetches one of the baby's napkins off the brass rail in front of the range, wets it in a jug, and starts dabbing at me face. Well, you know what it's like.

"I can wash me own face, Mam!"

"But yer all scabbed and clarted up! What did you say to him, Isaac? Whatever you said, there was no need for this."

"Give over, Mam. Give it here. Let me do meself!" I was grabbing the napkin off her. "And he didn't do it all. I fell against boot-scrape." By Christ, but me face was tender.

"Sulking int' stables like a wet cat, he said you were." Eh, I can just hear her. "As if we haven't had enough

24

troubles to bear . . ." she says. "And yer uncles being here and all . . ."

Well, me mother turned away from me, and I think she was trying not to cry. There's a gas-lamp hissing in the parlour, and the snap of one of my uncles dealing out playing cards, and me looking at my mother's thin back.

I wanted to go and put my arm round her, friendly, careless, like our Dan would have done. But I couldn't because of the dress she was wearing. That black shiny satin made her back look as hard as a beetle.

Across the hallway, my uncles were playing cards in the parlour.

"A pair of kings and a pair of jacks," that was my father's voice, and I'll tell yer, I flinched when I heard it. I was afraid she might send me in to see him.

But, at last, she says, "You give yer father some respect, Isaac Campion. Do you hear me? Now get away to bed. You can sleep in with Becca. But mind, yer to be up early for the horses. Yer father's had a word wi't school-board. Yer not going anymore. He wants you for the work. And there'll be work aplenty getting ready for the Irish mares, now we're without Dan."

So that's how I found out I was to leave school and work for my father. That's how I was told what I was expected to do for the rest of my life.

"But I've not had no supper, Mam," I says.

"And he says yer to have none. Oh Isaac, get to yer bed." She was having to do what my father said, you see. She couldn't stand up to him.

I went up the stairs in the dark. There was no electric light then. But I didn't go to bed. I sat on the top step, hugging my knees, wondering what the bloody hell I'd been born for. Aye, it was dark and all, except for a bit of light gleaming on the brass stair-rods.

And then downstairs someone went into the kitchen.

"Now then. Where's that nephew of mine?" And this was Uncle Harry. Uncle Harry who I liked.

"Oh Alice. Alice lass," he says. "Don't take on so . . ."

Well, I was listening to them. Eavesdropping. And now my mother was crying.

"But yer should have seen his face, Harry," she says.

"It's that bad, is it. I saw your Samuel's knuckles. Mind, he says he missed him on the second swing and walloped the door-jamb. Split his knuckles right open . . . He's sorry, Alice. That's what Sam said. He said, 'Harry, I'm sorry I hit him. It just got the better of me'. That's what he said." Uncle Harry was trying to comfort her, you see.

"Aye . . . but that's after," me mother says. "He does things and then he's sorry after. Oh Harry . . . You're his brother. Can't you stop all this?"

"I can't change his nature, lass," says Uncle Harry. "Here, come on now. Come on, here's me hankie. You blow your nose."

I could smell the smoke from his cigar coming up the stairwell, and I dare say I was getting a lump in me throat an' all.

"But it's not just Isaac," my mother says. "It's all of it . . . where's it to end? Where's it to end, Harry?"

"Here . . . what you need is a good drop of tonic wine. It's yer nervous constitution . . . And I'll tell you where it'll end," says me Uncle Harry. "It'll end where it always does. One day your Isaac'll be taller than his father's shadow, then – wallop! Sam'll find himself sitting on his backside, rubbing his chin in surprise. That'll put an end to it. Same as me and my old feller. That'll put an end to it. Here. Tuck this hair-pin back, it's got stuck in me sleeve."

"Put an end to it!" I've never heard my mother's voice sound so strange. "Put an end to it! You'll put them both on the end of a rope! Oh . . . get back to the parlour, Harry. You don't know what the 'nation I'm talking about."

You see, I wasn't the only one who could see trouble

26

looming. My mother could and all. What with the Laceys, and with me.

Talk to a lad these days, and mostly they want to leave school. They can't wait to be let out. Well, I suppose I did as well, but I'd seen a different world in that school-room. Maps of the Empire. History. Geography. Books. I'd had some secret fancy notions about what I was going to do with me life. But now I'd heard the gates of my future clang shut, so to say. I'd been shut in with the horses, like Dan.

There was none of this talk then about "What do you want to do when you grow up?" It was do what your father did, or get in the workhouse. It was do what your father did, or starve. I should have seen, I suppose, that I was luckier than most. At least my father was his own master. He wasn't a labourer. He was his own man. But all I could see was that he was to be *my* master, and there was no Daniel any more to stick up for me.

So this is what I was sitting on the stairs thinking. He's my father. And he's my master. And there's nowt in the future but the Devil or the deep blue sea.

Chapter Three

"Honour thy father and mother." "Whosoever curseth his father and mother, his lamp shall be put out in obscure darkness." At that time of day it was all bible texts everywhere, and you had them to learn. You'd to recite them at school. You had them to learn and you had them to believe. Even my father could quote chapter and verse at you, though he was trying to dodge the devil by not going to church.

Well, I'd got to thinking to myself, this is all very well and good, but what if there had been some mistake? *What if you'd got born to the wrong parents*? What if God had never intended you to be the son of this man? Then what?

And that's what I was thinking to myself at dawn, when I was lying in bed with our little Becca asleep at my back. That's how my mind was running along when footsteps come creaking down the landing, and my father puts his head round the door.

"Get theesel' shirted," he says. It wasn't even light. It was cold and grey and a while before sun up.

"Isaac!"

"Aye. I heard," I says. I was used to being woken at dawn, but I wasn't used to getting up then. It was our Daniel who would have to drag himself out of bed, and I'd roll into the big warm dent where Dan had been sleeping and close my eyes again, knowing I was safe for an hour or two yet. But that day, my father was expecting me to take Daniel's place in the stableyard, and I was damned if I could. I could not take Dan's place. I knew I would fail at it.

But I'd to pull my clothes on, and get myself out into the yard. And I'd be shivering and blowing clouds of breath into my hands.

There was no ceremony. This was my first real day of work. You could say, it was the day I'd to stop being a child and to start being a man. But my father never says owt. Not, "Na then, Isaac. We've had our troubles in the past, but now we've got to rub along together." No. Nothing like that.

It's straight out into the cold yard and, "Get yersel' up Crook's field. Yer to fetch down 'bald mare. And mind you lead her. I'm not having her aborting from you dancing about on her back." And that was all my father said.

He didn't say a word about our quarrel, though my cheek was swollen like toothache. He just gives me my orders, and goes on buttoning up his coat.

I can remember my father's hands. Great strong hands, he had, all covered in veins on the back just like the ribs on the underneaths of cabbage leaves. And his eyes were as blue as bonfire smoke.

So that was it. By the time the sun had come up over the edge of the moors behind Hardacre, I'd already walked two miles. I was on my way up Harrow Hill to fetch the piebald mare.

There was no talk of money, of being paid to work for him. He didn't expect to pay me. I was his son. My pay was the roof over my head, the food in my mouth, and the shirt on my back. I wouldn't have dared ask him for money, even if I'd thought about it.

I can remember the first time Daniel asked my father for money. He was eighteen when he died, and he'd be sixteen when this happened. That is to say, he'd already worked for my father for four years without asking for a penny. We were in the kitchen one evening, my father, my mother and me,

29

when Dan comes in. "Na then, Father," he says. "I want eleven shillings off thee." Eleven shillings! That was damn near the wage of a grown man, if he was a farm-hand, say.

My mother froze to the spot, and so did I. We were waiting for the explosion!

Me father pushed back his chair, and looked at Dan. "Eleven shilling? What do yer want it for?"

"I want to buy a hat," says Dan. "A man needs a hat to wear on his head."

"A hat'll not cost eleven shillings," says me father. "I'll give you three shilling and fourpence."

And Daniel smiled at the corner of his mouth. "Na then, Father," he says, "And what would you think of a man who wears a three and fourpenny hat but who's nowt in his pockets save his hands?"

Well, that makes my father laugh out loud, and he gave Dan the money! But that was the difference between me and my brother. Daniel had this way of dealing with my father. He had my father's dealing blood in him. And I didn't.

My father thought I was gormless, and he was right! He'd made me gormless with always shouting at me until I couldn't do anything for fear of doing it wrong.

So there's me, off up the hill in the cold dawn. And I didn't mind that, though it brought back some memories of being out with Dan. Sometimes I'd get up early and go with him, and he'd have his two dogs running at his heels. It would still be misty. There'd be mist hanging in the hollows of the fields, and you'd see the horses standing up to their bellies in mist before the sunrise. And I'd be thrilled to be out with my brother at that hour of day. Dan would be looking over the hedge, or over a gate, into the fields. Then, "There she sits!" he'd whisper. And I'd be looking, looking, looking.

"She's sat there," Dan would say. He had eyes like a hawk. He could spot a hare a mile away. Then, all of a sudden, I'd see the hare's lugs. Just the tips of her ears, poking out of the mist.

And Dan would have his hands on the collars of his dogs. They knew this was his signal. Then he'd let them go, and they'd be over the top of the gate, and the hare would be running for her life. But she wouldn't get far before she fell to them! It makes your blood run cold, does the cry of a hare.

But Dan would give me the hare to carry home to my mother. I'd to hide it in my shirt, and I'd be as proud as a king when I put it on the kitchen table. As proud as if I'd caught it myself!

Aye, well. That was all past. And I'd a lonely walk up Harrow Hill that May morning.

When I got to the field, I was in luck, because the piebald mare was standing watching me over the top bar of the gate, as if she'd been waiting for me. That meant I'd not have to play silly beggars chasing her round the field.

"Na then . . . Na then, lass," I says. Well, I'll tell you the truth – if you've not already guessed it. I was nervous of horses, mares and horses. I'd lived with them all my life, but I was still uneasy with them. And the worst thing was, they sensed it in me and played up. I was always that worried about doing something wrong, you see. I'd say that was the heart of the trouble.

That's not to say I didn't love them, because I did. I loved them, and most of all I loved to see all those unbroken yearlings and mares my father bought back from Ireland, galloping together in a field, bunching together like a shoal of great fish. I loved them when they were like that – brown and black, roan and piebald, all different shades of colour, running together, with the big muscles in their shoulders and their tails flicked high . . . Oh, I'd the wrong idea of horses to be working in my father's stableyard. I wanted to see them galloping away over the hills. My father wanted them broken to his command at the end of a long rein.

Well, at least I was in luck with that mare. "Na then . . ." I says, and she twitched an ear forward, hearing my voice, like she was pleased to see somebody. She was big-bellied with the foal she was carrying. So I slipped the halter on, tugged her forelock through, straightened her ears and fastened the knot on her cheek. And I felt right grateful to her for not playing up. But that's not how it should be. With a horse or a mare, you should not be feeling grateful if you're in my father's line of work. You should be the master. And the master doesn't feel grateful. He gets what he wants with his will.

Then me and the mare set off down the hill, and I only stopped for a minute where the lane slopes steeply down to the town, to see if I could see the Isle of Man.

People said it was sometimes possible to see that far from Harrow Hill. You could look down to the river, then out across the salt marshes to the bay, and then there'd be a bit of shining on the horizon, and that was the Irish Sea. They've built houses on Harrow Hill now, but I often had to go up there before Dan died. My mother would send me to look for the steamboat coming up the river. I'd to run down and tell her my father and the Irish horses were due in on the quayside. Aye, there was many a time I've stood on that hill, and my heart would sink when I saw the little grey steamboat far out in the estuary.

Well, because of the funeral, like I told you, my father hadn't gone that year, but we were expecting the boat any day.

No, I've not forgotten that first day of working for my father, nor what happened that evening at this conference of my uncles. I thought my life had changed when Daniel died, but I'd say it was the events of this day that shaped my destiny, so to say. It locked things between me and my father forever, and you can't go back in time and make it happen any different. So all I can do is tell you what went on.

When I'd put the mare in the back paddock, I went in for my breakfast. For a bite to eat. I'd not had any supper the night before, and hunger was gnawing my belly like a rat.

I remember, my Uncle Jack was sitting at the table with my father, but my Uncle Harry had taken the trap to the station. He'd gone to pick up my Uncle Howard.

When my Uncle Jack saw the bruise on my cheek, he whistled. "How's t'other feller?" he says, like it was a big joke.

But my mother pinned Uncle Jack with her eyes, then she fetched a plate of eggs for me out of the range. Well, I sat quiet and ate, chasing my eggs round the plate with my fork. I didn't want to say anything that might spark my father off, so I was just keeping my head down. But, I'll tell yer, I was inventing a civil conversation in me head! A conversation between me and my father, like, "Did she give yer any trouble, son?" "No, Dad, she were quiet as a lamb." "Grand. Get theesel' a good breakfast, then we'll set to, shall we?"

I'd have given my heart to my father, if he'd have just spoken like that to me once . . . I was no different to any other lad. I wanted his good opinion more than anything else in the world.

But they just went on talking as if I wasn't there. Only my mother kept giving me secret little smiles, as if she wanted to tell me something.

"Harry was telling me you've been doing some business wi' tramways, Sam," says Uncle Jack.

"Aye," says my father, stubbing a finger of bread into his egg yolk. "Six pair, Bill Grafton wanted. And not just any old pullers, but bloody show horses. Masterpieces of horses, Jack! Not what you'd call tramway's stock at all. Still, ask no questions."

"That's a queer do," says Uncle Jack. "I'd heard that the tramways were going electrified starting this year. They reckon there'll not be one horse left drawing a tram by

Christmas next year. Bill Grafton's got the job of getting *rid* of tramway livestock, not buying it . . ."

"And he's just bought them horses off yer?" my mother says, and my father starts frowning at his plate.

"And that's not all I heard," says Uncle Jack. "Though this I'll not vouch for. I heard yon Bill Grafton were courting Margaret Lacey, though what the hell he sees in her, the devil only knows!"

Most of this was just going in one ear and out the other, but I can remember thinking that the name of the Laceys seemed to stick in our house like a shadow. Wherever you went it followed you.

Any road, I was about to get a surprise on my own account. I wanted to wipe up the yolk off me plate, so I says, "Can I've a stop of bread, Mam?"

"Yer not having bread," she says.

Well, I couldn't believe me ears! I knew me and my father weren't getting on, but I couldn't believe this!

The next moment, my mother set a little curd cake on the table in front of me, and she was smiling. This cake was sprinkled with cinnamon, and fair drunk with raisins soaked in rum. And I'd asked her for bread! I didn't know what the hell was going on!

"What's that fer?" I says.

"It's fer thee," says me mother.

"What fer?" Well, it turns out she'd made it special because it was my first day at work. A little celebration. But from the look on my father's face, I could see she'd said nothing to him about it. He glanced up at me, looked hard at her, then just went on mopping the egg yolk off his plate with a crust. And as for me Uncle Jack, he was keeping well out of all this.

I was almost too nervy to touch it. My mother's trying to keep on smiling, and I think she must have been hoping that my father would say something. That he'd take this chance to make up his quarrel with me. Oh, it was some celebration was that! I felt bitterly sorry for my mother, trying to make it a little occasion for me, and no one else joining in.

My father reaches for the teapot. "Get it eaten," he says. "There's work to do." Then he turned to my Uncle Jack. "He made as much a masterpiece of coming into this world as he is of getting yon cake down his neck. I remember it yet, Jack. I thought I'd have to tie a rope round his heels and drag him out like a calf!"

"Samuel! God alive! What a thing to say and me and the child present in yer hearing!" cries my mother.

"Why not? You were present then an' all."

It went quiet as ice in the kitchen. He'd deliberately shamed her in front of my Uncle Jack.

"Come on, Isaac," my mother says at last. "Get yer cake eaten." But all the pleasure had been knocked out of her.

I couldn't have eaten a morsel to save my life. I'd have choked.

"Can I not save it?" I says.

"You can do what the hell you like with it, lad," my father says, pushing his chair back. "But yer to take that old bully-beef nag in the far stables down to the slaughteryard after. So think on. When you've been to Harry Black's you might not have stomach for eating owt at all." Then he fetched his watch out of his pocket, and says, "Harry should be back from the station wi' Howard by half-past. That just gives us time to get over to the tramways depot. I want a word with yon Bill Grafton!" Then he turned back to me.

"And yer to tell Harry Black I want six bob for that carcase and not a farthing less. And when yer get back, there's harnesses and brasses want rubbing up."

Now here is a strange thing. You can go on forgiving someone for what they do to you. It's amazing how you can go on forgiving someone for the rough way they treat you. But what you can't forgive is the way they hurt someone else. And my father had hurt my mother about this cake, just as

35

surely as if he'd slapped her face, and there was nowt I could do.

I had to do what he said. My father told you to do something and you'd to jump and do it. And you dare not say no! Well, you'd to jump to them both. But I would jump for my father quicker than I would for my mother perhaps, because he'd a domineering way with him and a hard hand! But you didn't do what he asked willingly. There was no pleasure in doing a job for him.

To be fair, I would say he didn't know how hard he treated us. I would say he treated me the way his father, my grandfather Reuben Campion, had treated him. And old Reuben Campion *was* a hard man. I know that for a fact, because my Uncle Harry told me what a hard man my grandfather was.

I went from that table with my heart burning like a coal. I took the old mare down to Harry Black's slaughteryard – and that is not a place I shall dwell on. That was an evil place for a boy to try and lead a living creature into, for the mare would get wind of the slaughteryard even before you turned in at Harry Black's gate. And you might have to lead her past the carcase of another horse, with its legs stuck up in the air like wagon-shafts. And a man like Harry Black didn't care how he treated the beasts that came in through his gate. He wasn't slaughtering for the table, so he didn't care if he bruised the meat.

Well, I came back to the stableyard, and my heart was burning like a lump of coal, but then I'd all the harnesses to clean. There were five sets of harness, and whatever else my father had in to sell. And every piece of harness – and it isn't everybody that can take them to pieces and put them back together again – every scrap had to be taken to pieces, and had to be cleaned thoroughly. And when it was done, my father would inspect it before it could be hung back up on its nails. There would always be something for him to find fault with. It was a job that even used to drive our Daniel to the wall.

By the end of that afternoon, my heart and my hands were both black – one with bad feeling against my father, and the other with the dubbin and oil I'd used on the leather, and the ashes I'd used to rub up the brass.

And I'll tell you what I think it was, why those men were like that. They'd got it from religion. And I'm not talking about the religion of love. I'm talking about the Old Testament. The Bible of masters and work. "Spare the rod and spoil the child", and pleasure was a sin. My great-grandfather had beaten that into my grandfather, and my father had had it beaten into him. And he couldn't even take pleasure in his own son having a bit of curd cake!

But there was not one of those men lived to see sixty! Not my father nor my uncles! Apart from Uncle Harry, and he saw eighty and a day, and I would say I followed after him.

But by the end of my first day of working for my father, my heart had turned black against him, and I wanted to turn the tables. And this is a terrible state for a young lad to be in. I wanted to get my own back. And I did do, that very night at the gathering of my uncles, because that was the night I raised Dan's ghost.

Chapter Four

As I TOLD YOU BEFORE, none of us had seen Uncle Howard Brank for at least four years. And if it hadn't been for the fact that Uncle Harry drove into the yard with him, we wouldn't have recognised him. We would not have known him from Adam! I'd remembered him as a hard muscled man, but Uncle Howard Brank had got fat.

There he was, in the parlour after supper, standing by my mother's best polished table, topping up his whisky with water, but the glass disappeared into his fist like an egg wrapped in sausage meat. Oh aye, a right slabby lump of lard our family prize-fighter had become! Belly on him. Double chin. Back side like a pig's arse!

Now this was a turn-up for the books. My father had been expecting Uncle Howard to chair the lynch-mob, as you might say. He'd expected him to come along and sort out Clem Lacey and Dick Lacey with a couple of jaw-crackers! Instead, there was Uncle Howard in a showman's check jacket, as fat and drunk as a farmer on Hiring Day.

And this happens to boxers sometimes, when they get older. All that muscle on them turns to flab and lard. And their brains have got that rattled in their heads from all the punching and slamming, they get a bit addled. Oh, it's a sad thing to see, right enough.

Well, I crept onto the window-seat to listen, with those thick red curtains pulled round me like an Arab in a tent.

But as soon as I'd gone into the parlour, I'd felt the climate.

Uncle Jack and Uncle Harry kept glancing at each other, and Uncle Howard was standing there, gabbing away, pouring whisky down his fat throat. And my father was glaring into the fire.

Name o' God, but Uncle Howard was gabbing on! Talk, talk, talk! It was like listening to my mother's turkey-cock, and he didn't seem to feel this climate building up.

There was a couple of stuffed jays – birds my father had shot and had mounted in a glass case – and even they seemed to be staring at him with their glass eyes!

Oh, it was a right old-fashioned room was our parlour. Prints of horses on the walls, copper coal scuttle, a brass pot with a green plant in, and my father's gun in a rack by the door.

On goes Uncle Howard, gabbing nonsense. "You know what my old mother used to say? You remember what my old mother used to say, eh? Samuel? Howard, she used to say, you were born with no teeth at a very early age – and yer tongue still fills yer mouth! And yer tongue still fills yer mouth! Eh, she were a cob 'un, God rest her . . ." And Uncle Howard's beaming at everyone with his eyes watering over his whisky, but no one was smiling back.

Now then, Isaac, I says to meself. Here's a bit of fun! Oh, it filled me with glee. My father wasn't getting what he wanted. He was sulking by the fire.

And the only other person who seemed to be seeing the funny side was my Uncle Harry. He was sitting there, with his long legs stretched out, and a little hook of a smile on the corner of his mouth. Watching it all. Just the corner of his mouth turned down. And every now and again he'd raise his eyebrow at Uncle Jack, or look across the room at me and wink. That look on his face – it reminded me of our Dan.

Well, at last, my father's had enough. He turns his back on Uncle Howard and tries to get down to business. "Me and

Jack went over to the tramway depot this morning, Harry," he says. "And I was right. There *is* summat brewing up between Bill Grafton and Clem Lacey."

Uncle Harry just goes on running his finger round the rim of his glass, making it hum.

And Uncle Jack says, "Sam, how the hell do yer know anything's up. Bill Grafton hardly give us more than top o' morning and time o' day."

Me father damn near leapt out of his chair. "I know the ins and outs of William Grafton!" he yells. "I bloody well know when summat's up! I've been dealing wi' him half me life. I know when summat's up!"

Well, that made us all jump a bit! But it didn't do my father any good, shouting like that at his brothers and his brother-in-law. He might get away with yelling at me and my mother, but he'd not get away with it with them. It's the same with any family. One starts shouting, and the others harden up against him. They close ranks.

There's me, peeping between the curtains, and I suddenly saw what was going on. It was a revelation! As far as my uncles were concerned, there was nowt to be afraid of! There'd not be any talk o' murder. They'd not help my father do owt that was wild. No, no, no. He was in it by himself! They didn't give a damn about the Laceys. The Laceys meant nowt to them.

Well, it made me want to laugh out loud. With relief, like. But it was strange, and all, to see my father out on a limb like that.

The table kept creaking as Uncle Jack shifted his backside against it, and there's Uncle Howard squeezed into a chair just like a lump of dough slobbering over the edge of a crock. They'd not do nowt! They looked a bit fed up with my father's frowning.

Only my Uncle Harry looks hard at my father for a long stretch of minutes. And it's like he's looking at a sick man. "How about a hand of baccarat, Samuel?" he says. "I can always think better with a pack of cards in my hand. Fetch 'em down off mantelshelf, Jack. Let's play for a thrupenny stake."

That's what he did, did Uncle Harry. He just changed the subject and set up a card game and handed my father one of his cigars. Well, my father wasn't happy about it. But what could he do?

I leant back against the window, almost grinning to meself. That day, my heart had hardened against my father, you see, and it made me smile to see that he wasn't getting it all his way.

Dick-William's lamp goes wobbling across the yard, and I heard the gate clang to as he set off for the *The Turk's Head*. Stars were coming out over the stable roof, and the tassles of the curtains were swaying in the draught from the door. They were like red spiders, the tassles on those curtains. I've never forgotten them. And I'd be falling asleep. I'd been up since dawn, and I was weary to the bone. In fact, I'd say I nearly was asleep, when I blinked and, suddenly, I was eye to eye with something looking in through the glass!

Yell! Yer damn right I yelled! I fell off bloody window seat, and the men all leapt to their feet, cards going everywhere!

"What's to do wi' yer? What's tha doing there, lugging?" my father shouts. "Get away to yer bed!"

"I saw summat!" I was shaking all over, and my heart's thundering like a flaming waterwheel.

"What's to do, lad?" says Uncle Harry. "You look like yer've seen a boggart."

"I saw summat, looking in!" I says.

"What?" My father grabs for his shotgun, and Uncle Jack grabs for the door.

"I never heard dogs," says Uncle Harry.

"I've no dogs anymore. They were Dan's. I sold them. I'd no stomach for their pining."

"God alive, Sam! You want to get some dogs. Anyone

41

could creep into the yard. You could be murdered in yer beds!" And Uncle Harry goes out after them, still in his shirt sleeves, with the silky back of his waistcoat catching the light. And he still had his cards fanned out in his hand.

Well, I was staring out of the window into the night. And it was dawning on me who had been out there. I could not believe it. He must have been mad to come into our yard. He must have heard that my uncles were here, and wanted to know what they were planning. It was *Dick Lacey*, do you follow me? It was Dick Lacey, crouched under the window, eavesdropping. The lad that had dared our Daniel to jump.

I'd not thought about it like this before. But ever since the day our Dan had died, that young lad must have lived in a rare state o' mortal fear.

Well, I couldn't catch me breath. It was like Dan all over again. How can I explain it to you? One minute everything was all right, and the next . . .

Any second, I expected to hear me father's gun go off! I had to do something, you see? But it was like I was frozen to the spot, hearing them all outside.

"I can't see a damn thing!"

"There's nowt over here!"

"Christ Almighty, will yer fetch a lamp, Howard!"

"Is that you, Harry? No, I've looked int' stables."

"Well I'm damned to Huddersfield if I can see owt!"

I had to do something before they found him. So I ran to the door and yelled out, "It's no good looking! He's gone!"

"Who's gone, Isaac?" says Uncle Harry.

"Blast it all, I've torn me shirt." That was Uncle Jack.

But it was my father who came over and grabbed me by the arm. He was still carrying his gun. "Who's gone? You tell truth now, yer hear? You tell me the bloody truth, lad!"

I don't know why I said it. I don't know what possessed me. It just came into my head. "It was our Daniel!" I yelled into his face. "It were Dan, and he was shaking his head at thee!"

He snatched his hand from me as if I'd turned into a snake. As if I'd bitten him.

Nobody said a word. Not even Uncle Harry. We just stood in the black yard with only a bit of light from the lamp in my mother's bedroom window flickering over our heads. And what I'd shouted seemed to keep echoing in the silence. And the way I shouted it, even I half-believed what I'd said for a minute.

That was the blackest lie I ever told in my life. It stabbed my father to the heart. It jumped out of my mouth like a demon. And I shall have it to answer for on Judgement Day. It was a sin against the dead and the living to raise my brother's ghost.

Come next morning, and I was up at dawn, helping Dick-William back Uncle Jack's horse between the shafts of his trap. Uncle Jack and fat Uncle Howard were leaving.

I don't know what they had all talked about after I'd gone away to my bed, but it must have been something deep. They had believed what I'd said. They had believed that the ghost of their nephew had been watching them through the parlour window. It had put the wind up them. It must have been the final straw. They hadn't wanted to get involved with my father's quarrel with Clem Lacey in the first place, but to have Daniel's ghost shaking his head at them, well, that was the final straw.

So, at dawn, two of my uncles took their leave. They hardly said a word – just drove off through the gateway, and the iron rims on the wheels of the trap went rumbling off along the cobbled street. I watched them go. It was a very still morning at that early hour, just a bit of grey sunlight and the cobbles still wet. Then it seemed very quiet in the stable-yard.

They'd not mentioned what I'd seen, but my father had collared me on the stairs when I came out of the bedroom. He looked very haggard, as if he'd hardly slept.

43

"Don't breathe a word about last night to yer mother . . ." he said.

All through that day and the next, my father kept glancing at me. Looking at me when he didn't think I was watching. And when Uncle Jack and Uncle Howard had vanished down the street, he'd stood for a long time at the gate, staring out. Just staring away at nothing, gnawing the fringe of his moustache.

Oh, he was troubled to his very soul all right. You might think it would have pleased me to see him troubled like that. Gleeful, to have turned the tables on him. But it didn't. I felt what I'd said was like blasphemy. I was afraid I might really have disturbed the dead.

Aye, it had subdued my father right enough, at least for the time being. I kept catching him watching me across the yard with a strange look on his face, as if it wasn't his son that he was seeing, but summat queer and strange. Summat as queer as a white crow.

I didn't like that, but I got the feeling he'd not lay a finger on me for a long while. *I* was used to being scared of *him*, but for a day or so, the tables were turned. It gave me a jolt, and it wasn't a pleasant feeling. Oh no . . . it was a jolt.

I was very glad that Uncle Harry was still in the house.

Any road, after they'd left, I'd the mucking out to do, and I was glad to hide away in the stables. It was calm in there, forking dung and straw onto the hand-cart. Oh, it was quiet all over the yard that dawn. Even Dick-William was keeping his head down and his mouth shut, as if he could sense summat new was in the air. But it wasn't a calm quiet. It was like waiting for a storm.

And I'd some new thinking to do as I went about my work. All that time since the funeral I'd been scared of what my father might do to Dick Lacey or to Clem Lacey. But I'd not been afraid for *them*, so to say. I'd not seen it from their point of view. I'd been scared for me, and for my mother and little Becca and baby Lizzy. For what might happen to us if

44

he did something that bloody daft. But now, I *was* thinking about Dick Lacey. That white face pressed up to the glass, looking at me. And I began to see the fear that lad must have been living in and all. It made me shiver for him, just to think about it.

Right down in the pit of my guts I wanted to weep. For him. For Dan. For myself. For the whole pity of it, I suppose. That was the word for it. It was pity, like I'd never felt it before.

I can remember stroking the shoulder of a gelding that was in one of the stalls, and feeding him wisps of fresh hay. Stroking him for me own comfort, like.

But I couldn't stop in there for ever. I'd work to do. I'd the stone troughs – drinking troughs for the horses – to clean out. They'd get full of black rotting leaves in the winter, and then green with slime when the warmer weather set in. You had them to keep clean and fresh.

Well, I scrubbed out one and refilled it. Then I scrubbed out the other, and I was working in a blind sort of way, with all these new feelings in my chest. All the while Dick-William was whistling, ever so quietly, *Our Captain Cried All Hands* as he went about his own jobs. I've never been able to hear that tune since, without getting a tight feeling across me chest . . .

Anyhow, it was after I'd scrubbed that second trough, and my arms were aching from lugging bucket after bucket of water from the pump, that something caught me eye. Down at the back of the trough. And I'll tell you what it was. It was a whistle – a little dog-whistle carved out of bone. And it had a fancy knot of initials carved on it – RL. Just those initials. Richard Lacey. RL.

Well, I knew then that this was where Dick Lacey must have hidden himself the night before, when my father and my uncles were searching the yard. He must have been crouched down there, in fear of his life, between the trough and the wall.

45

I was just looking at this whistle in my hand, when Uncle Harry calls to me. "By Christ," he says, "but you put yer back into that job, lad. Watching yer's quite wore me out!"

Uncle Harry was in the yard by the kitchen window. His shaving mirror was propped on the sill, and he was naked to the waist.

Well, I quickly hid this whistle in my pocket. "We've got to get ready for the Irish mares coming in," I says. "The boat's due in tomorrow." To this day, I'm sure he saw what I'd found. At least, I'd say, he had seen I'd found something that I didn't want anyone else to see.

But, "Oh aye," he says, pushing his nose to one side with his thumb so's he could shave round his moustache. And he was squinting sideways at me in his mirror. "Irish mares, eh?" Then he turns his face to scrape off the soapy whiskers on the other cheek.

"Well then," he says. "That should keep yer father busy, Isaac. That should keep him busy. That should keep his mind off things." He stopped to wipe the stubble and lather off the long blade of his razor, and he was watching me in the glass. You know, a long considering sort of look.

And there's me shifting guiltily, with this little whistle getting hot and slippery in my pocket, because I'm clutching it that tight. I was afraid he might ask me about Daniel's ghost. If anyone was going to ask – it was him. And if he'd have asked, I've a feeling I would have blurted the truth to him. In fact, I'm sure I would have done.

"Now then," he says, "here comes the tricky bit!" and he winked at me. Well, even the state I was in, I fair held me breath watching the way he curved that cut-throat razor to his cheekbone to put a neat edge to his sideburn. It made you hold your breath to watch him.

"Took me a long time to get the hang o' that," he says. "I could do left side right enough. But when it come to t'other I'd damn near slash me throat! You mark my words, Isaac – you leave off shaving as long as yer can."

"I'll grow a girt beard," I says.

"Will you now. You'll grow a bush beard, eh?" Oh he had this quiet mocking way of speaking. Gentle, though. I wished there and then, on the spot, that he was my father. He puts the razor down on the window ledge and splashes his face in the bowl of water. "And who's to say a man shouldn't grow a bush beard and look like a navvy if he wants to, eh?" He smooths his hand over his chin, looking from side to side in the mirror, smooths his moustache with his fingertips, then he turns to me again. That long, considering, thoughtful look, until I had to look away.

"Irish mares," he says. "Well, Isaac, let's hope that keeps yer father's mind off things . . ."

They had a saying in those days – a superstition. "Whistle for a wind," they'd say. I suppose, with the river being tidal and boats coming and going, this superstition had come from the sailors and the fishermen. And those men that work on the sea, they are a superstitious breed. And a fisherman would land you a clout across the ear if he heard you whistling on the quayside. It was bad luck! "I'll have yer! Whistling up a storm!" and that fisherman would fetch you a clout!

Well, I'm not saying I was doing any whistling that day. But I was walking round with Dick Lacey's whistle hidden in my pocket. And here is a strange thing. Though it had been a quiet dawn when my uncles drove away, come the afternoon and the weather had changed. The wind comes rattling and gusting round the yard, blowing all the petals off my mother's damson trees in the orchard. Petals were flying about like snow, and bits of hay and straw were twirling over the cobbles. And the worst thing about a gusting wind like that is – it tires you out.

I can remember me and Dick-William were struggling about our jobs in the yard. The wind would fetch you a buffet across the ear as hard as any fisherman's fist. Your shirt's ballooning across your back. You'd be leaning into the wind, trying to get across the yard to the stables, then suddenly the wind would drop, and you'd damn near fall flat on your face!

Oh, it was giving me jip. I'm not superstitious now, but I would say I was then. I lived in superstitious times. And I felt a right Jonah, with that whistle in my britches.

And it gives you an eerie feeling at the best of times – a dry wind suddenly coming up out of a still day.

Mind, me and Dick-William got out of it for a time. There was a bay gelding with a sour foot – with an infection. And this was more trouble for my father, because he'd a buyer interested in this gelding as part of a complete turn-out he was selling. That's to say, this horse was part of the deal – eight-year-old gelding, and a hansom cab with leather upholstery, rubber tyres, and a complete set of carriage lamps. No money had changed hands yet, and if the animal went lame – well, the buyer might back off. A cab's no use without a horse to pull it.

And money was getting short. He'd reached too deep in his pocket for Dan's funeral, had me father. He was banking on the Irish mares, and he needed a few deals to tide us over.

So, Dick-William and me got out of the wind and into the quiet stables. I'd to help our stableman sort this horse out. He'd to brew up an ointment for the bad hoof. He was a good man in that way – sulphur, pigs' fat, neatsfoot oil. He carried a fair old encyclopaedia of recipes around in his head, did Dick-William.

Well, the wind's banging and moaning round the yard, and I'm crouched in the stall, glad to be hiding from it, and glad to be out of the way of my father because he won't look me in the eye. But then he comes into the stable, and a gust of wind must have whipped the stable door out of his hand, and it slammed shut. It cracked shut and broke a hinge. Gelding starts! Kicks out at the planks of the stall, and

48

nearly kicks Dick-William in the face! But to make it worse –
me father yells at the horse. Shouts at it, and strikes it!

That gave me and Dick-William a shock. I'd never heard
my father raise his voice in the stables. Horsemen move
quietly about their animals in the stables. It's the best way.
It's a habit that gets in their blood. My father might yell his
lungs blue in the house – but not in the stables. And you do
not strike a frightened animal. You calm it. There's many a
good horse been ruined by being struck when it's frightened.

Well, Dick-William was gawping at him over the ointment
pot, and then my father saw that I was with the gelding as
well. He'd not realised I was there. And by shouting and
hitting out like that, he'd shamed himself in front of me. He
took one look at me, and turned away, he could not face me.
He couldn't bear seeing me.

"And who's to mend that hinge?" says Dick-William.
"That's what I want to know." By which he meant, me
father had broken it, and me father could damn well mend
it!

But I must have had a look on my face, because Dick-
William reached out his hand and gives my shoulder a
squeeze. "Steady up, lad," he says. "Steady up . . ." he says.
And he was soothing me in his own way. In his language of
horses.

Aye . . . that is a language you will not hear the day. Those
times are past forever. And there was no grander sight than
to see a man plough a straight black furrow up a field of
oat-stubble, with a two-horse hitch of Clydesdales. And to
hear the soft commands of that man come floating back
across the field, "Wook on, Captain. Wook on, Major." And
all the white birds following behind.

Well, any road, that blustering black wind kept blowing.
In the parlour, smoke was blowing back down the chimney
and gusting up over me mother's best brass candlesticks in
green sooty clouds. And my mother would weep for that soot
in the house, because it is a great spoiler.

And by the time Uncle Harry came strolling back from town, the rain had started pelting down. I can remember him having to run across the yard in his best top-coat, trying to dodge the rain drops. And shortly afterwards, my father came into the yard, leading a Clydesdale mare – one of these great plough horses I was just telling you about. The rain was pelting down on them as they came clap-clopping in through the gate, and the wind was rippling about her white, feathery, heavy feet, and the rain was streaming off her mane and off me father's hair, and his head was bent.

I can remember watching him from the kitchen door. I'd just come down stairs because I'd been hiding Dick Lacey's whistle behind the bedding chest.

And I can remember how bent and small he looked beside that great mare. The big man. My father. And he was soaked to the bone.

Chapter Five

UNCLE HARRY did his best that evening. I'll give him his due. He was like a cork was Uncle Harry. Like a cork in water. You could push him down, but up he'd come again.

We'd be having our supper together in the kitchen, all sat round the long table. The new baby would be in her wooden cradle by the range, and my mother had to keep an eye on the cradle. There was one of the stable cats that was a beggar for climbing in that cradle. It would sleep on the baby. And Becca would be on my mother's knee.

But my father's mood had hushed the whole house. He was just picking at his meal, and it made it hard for me and my mother to eat. Well, as I said, Uncle Harry did his best, making remarks, trying to start a civil conversation.

"Dick-William was saying you've got Tom Makepeace bringing his stallion over tomorrow, for yon Clydesdale mare. Reckoning to sell her in foal, Sam?"

"Aye," says my father. But he doesn't even look up.

"I was looking at a fancy colt not long back," says Uncle Harry. "A flashy blonde little chap he was, sired by one o' these Belgian stallions."

"Oh aye," says my father. It was like getting blood out of a stone. But Uncle Harry won't give up.

"Tom Makepeace, eh? Nay, they don't make 'em like him these days. He's a relic of times past. Tramping county wi' his stallion and his bull." And that's how Uncle Harry went on, until in the end he said something about how old Jed Henshaw, the horse doctor, had passed away in the night.

Well, that seemed to stir my father a bit, and he says, very quietly, as if he'd forgotten me and my mother and Becca were there, "I had a awful bad dream last night, Harry."

"Did yer?"

"I did, aye."

My heart came into my throat. I thought he was going to say something about Daniel.

There was a long bit of silence, and Uncle Harry's fork was scraping on his plate.

"I dreamed yon piebald mare in the paddock had foaled."

"That doesn't sound like a bad dream, Samuel," says my mother.

"I'm telling yer. It was a bad dream . . ."

His voice was that quiet, it made you listen. You had to listen to it.

"This foal – it were born wi'out skin. Wi'out hair nor hide. It was just all red muscle-meat and vitals, and I could see teeth of it, grinning in its skull . . ."

"Lord have mercy!" cries my mother, staring at him.

"What could that be a warning of, Harry?" says my father. "What could that mean?"

"It means you drank too much black tea afore yer went to yer bed," Uncle Harry says. "That's what it means, Sam. Too much black tea. It's bad for your constitution. You want to put a drop o' milk in it, like a civilised man."

"You're fretting, Samuel," says my mother. "That's all. I wish you'd stop fretting – you'll wear yoursel' down."

"I'm not fretting, Alice!" My father bangs his fork down on the table, making us all jump, and little Becca opens her mouth to cry.

"Na then, Samuel," Uncle Harry says. "I'll tell you what. We'll get across to the quay tonight – go down *The Crown and Anchor* and have a livener of good beer, eh?"

Well, my mother was about to say her piece about that.

52

She hated the drink. She was feared of strong liquor. But my Uncle Harry stops her with a look.

"And we can find out when the boat's due in tomorrow. The shipping list should be posted up outside custom's house by now. What do yer reckon?"

"Aye," says my father. "Aye, all right . . . I could do wi' a sup of beer . . . I don't know about yon steamboat. If it's blowing like this on the sea, I doubt but they'll sit it out in Douglas . . . Harry," he says. "It were as real as you sitting there. New born foal on its wobbly legs, wi'out a scrap of skin."

"Hush yer," my mother says. "Hush now, Samuel. You'll frighten the child."

Aye, he'd be very suspicious of that dream, would my father. And it was the weather to be suspicious in! It was blowing a gale. It had started blowing a gale from the moment I found Dick Lacey's whistle, so I was getting very jittery and all. I was thinking it was my fault for finding it, for whistling it up. And we'd a cargo of horses coming the next day.

And I'll tell you what else my father was suspicious of, a crowing hen. A crowing hen's unlucky! Oh, it happens sometimes. You'll get a hen that crows like a cock. And I've seen my father take a horse-whip to a crowing hen. Its head would come clean off. And that was it. "Unlucky bird," he'd say. "I'll not go out today!"

Well, this wasn't just my father. This was a lot of men. They had these superstitions, and really I'd say they were a load of bloody nonsense! But perhaps there was a pinch of truth in some of it.

I can remember this old horse-doctor, Jed Henshaw. He had a bit of a shack, a little hovel of a house, at the end of Robin Lane. And every morning he'd come out of his shack with hardly a stitch of clothing on him – just enough to cover his decency, so to say – and he'd stand in a patch of nettles. He'd give himself a good nettling, and he used to do this even when he was an old man. It was quite a comical sight!

"And what yer doing that fer, Mr Henshaw?" we'd say.

"As long as I'm getting nettled, I'll not suffer from the rheumatics, my child," he'd say. And he never did! He died when he was ninety-one, and he'd walked eleven mile to tend a sick mare on that very day!

Well, off went my father and Uncle Harry into that howling black night. I'd to fetch in a hod of coal, and then I stayed in the kitchen with my mother. She'd put baby Lizzy on my lap, and I can remember the way Lizzy would kick the palms of my hands with her naked pink feet. I'd press my hands against the soles of the baby's feet, and she'd laugh and kick. And my mother would be struggling with Becca.

Becca had been coughing and sneezing and mithering all that winter. And my mother was trying to wipe Becca's tongue with paste swabs. Swabs she'd make up from flour and salt and lemon juice, to stop this cold getting on her chest. Becca would spit and sob, until my mother would end up kneeling on the rug with her, rocking and hugging her in her arms, and singing soft little songs into her hair.

And all the while the wind's howling in the chimneys and rattling the windows. Then something started banging in the yard.

"'Nation!" says my mother. "Go and see to it, Isaac. Happen it's the coal-house door. Yer've left it open."

"I've not, Mam. I closed it."

"Go and see to it."

So I'd to pass the baby over to her, and go out into the dark with a lamp. And I don't know if you've ever noticed this. If you cup your hand round the chimney of a lamp, or round a candle flame, you can see all the blood in your fingers, and the shadow of your finger-bones under the skin. Brr! It reminded me of me father's dream!

Well, that banging was coming from the gateway, not the coal-house. It was one of the gates swinging open, and clanging in the wind. Oh, it was a rough night. There was no one about on the street, nothing at all but the yellowish cloud of light round the gas-lamp on the corner. And I'd just shut the gate and turned back to the house, when this black shadow goes leaping behind the beech tree at the bottom of our yard.

I was that frightened, I nearly dropped the lamp. I was thinking of Daniel's ghost, you see. But then the fear went. I don't know. Perhaps deep down, I'd been expecting this. There's the branches of the beech tree hushing and roaring by the gate-post, but I knew who was standing behind that tree. He'd come back for his whistle.

"Dick? Dick?" I whispers. "Dick Lacey? I've found yer whistle, Dick. I've got it hid."

"Why didn't yer give me away?" a voice whispers back, and then Dick Lacey stepped out from behind the tree.

"Ah knew it were thee!" I says. "Yer musn't come here. He'd throttle yer, Dick." I was afraid for him! I was afraid me father might come along the street! "He'd shoot yer like a fox."

There he stood, just on the edge of my lamplight, a tall thin lad of sixteen, with the necks of a couple of bottles sticking out of his pocket like the ears of a hare. And the wind was buffeting him, and the shadows of the lamp were leaping about. He looked like nothing more than a bundle of black cloth wrapped round a stick.

"Did they believe yer?" he whispers. "Daniel's ghost?"

That gave me a jolt. He must have heard what I'd yelled at my father. He'd been hiding down all the time by the trough.

"Aye, they did," I says. And I was sorry for it. That lie was haunting my father, and it was haunting me.

"I've come back for my whistle . . . I knew I'd dropped it but I couldn't find it in the dark."

"It's hidden safe," I says.

And then Dick Lacey came closer, and he says, "I wanted to come to Dan's funeral. No, listen to me, Isaac Campion. Listen to me. No beggar else will. I *wanted* to come. Me and Daniel – we were just larking about. You saw. You saw it, Isaac. Your Dan half murdered me once when we were little lads. In a scrap. Bloody Laceys and Campions, same as always, in a scrap! It's daft. We were quite friendly after that. We never let on, though."

Well, he touches my arm, and he's whispering, and I'd say I felt sorry for him.

"I told my father I were coming to t' funeral, and to hell wi' what you lot might do. He knocked me down . . ."

"I got clouted an' all," I says. "Can you see the bruise on me face?"

"Aye," he says. "I guessed it were summat. I didn't mean to kill yer brother, Isaac. I didn't."

"Isaac!" my mother had come to the back door. She was wondering where I'd got to.

"Hush, Dick," I hissed at him. "Ah must go. I'll fetch yer whistle. Not now. I can't do it now. I'll fetch it tomorrow, about four o'clock. Makepeace's stallion is covering a mare then. I'll slip out."

"Isaac! What's to do?" my mother's calling.

"It's just the gate, Mam!" I yelled. "Meet yer under first pillar of Kingdom Bridge. Quick, get going! She's coming out!"

So Dick Lacey slipped out through the gate, and I closed it after him, just as my mother comes up with a shawl wrapped round her shoulders and her hair straggling in the wind.

"Is the bolt stuck?" she says.

"Aye. It was, but I jigged it loose," I says. Lying beggar.

I was glad to have talked to him. Does that seem strange to you? It seems strange to me. But that's how it was. I was glad he'd come. And I couldn't wait to give his whistle back. I

56

was impatient to get it off me hands. I'd half a notion, you see, that when I gave him his whistle back the wind would drop, and this gale would die away.

Come the next morning, and the wind had dropped a bit, and we'd be taking notice of this, you see, because the boat was due in that evening. But it never seemed to get properly light. There'd be great splashes of sunshine bursting over the yard, then you'd be back under the black belly of a cloud.

Well, I'd my usual chores to do, and then I spent most of the day helping Dick-William and my father get things ready for the stallion. Usually we'd take a mare over to Tom Makepeace's but, for some reason, on that day Tom Makepeace came over to us.

And I expect my father was cursing a bit, that this mare should be giving him the wink on the same day that the boat was due in. That's how a mare tells you she's ready for the stallion, because she winks at you under her tail, so to speak. And you've to count the days between this happening.

Oh, it's not a kiss-me-quick business. We'd quite a lot to do before Tom Makepeace arrived with his stallion. There was what Dick-William called his 'tryst-board' to set up – and that is a sturdy fence over which the mare and the stallion could meet and do their courting. If the mare gets wicked and isn't ready for that stallion, it helps keep them apart, you see.

And then there was what Dick-William used to call his 'opera box' to set up in the yard. And that's a narrow, three sided box made of strong planks and poles, for the mare to stand in while the stallion covers her.

So we'd these jobs to get on with. It all needed doing right, because the mating of heavy horses can be a risky business. You've to remember what those great horses can weigh. Well, I'll tell you a story about that. Tom Makepeace, this stallioner, had only his forefinger and his thumb left on his right hand. He'd lost the other three in one

57

moment's carelessness when an unready mare had turned vicious. And with only those two fingers left on it, Tom Makepeace's hand looked just like the head and beak of some horrible bald-headed vulture! It always made me shudder to look at it.

Well, come three o'clock, we'd everything ready, and I was left to tear up a piece of linen into strips, or bandages, to bind the mare's tail, to keep it out of the stallion's way, and out of the men's way in case the stallion was clumsy and needed helping in. And all the while I was planning me escape. I'd to go and meet Dick Lacey, you see.

Well, my father had changed into his best black top-coat and a smart black bowler, and even Dick-William had dusted himself off a bit, and he'd be rubbing up the nap on his hat with his sleeve. It was quite an occasion, having the stallion there. Everyone would dress up a bit.

Well, along comes Tom Makepeace with his big clop-clapping stallion, and my mother hurries out of the house with glasses of port wine on a little tray.

And I'll tell you something else. It was said that apart from one finger of drink to toast the serving, not a single drop of liquor passed between Thomas Makepeace's lips from April to October every year, though he spent the whole frosty winter blind roaring drunk! Aye, he was a big block of a man, with a broad red face and teeth like piano keys, but a more mild-tempered man you couldn't hope to meet. At least, when he was sober, that is.

Well, my father and he shake hands, and I can hear the church clock striking the hour. I was just waiting for my chance to slip away while the men went to inspect the mare through the stable door.

"She's not so bad, but she's a cob-looking flash on her face. It makes her look as if she's squinting," says my father.

"Aye, well," says big Tom Makepeace, and he spits peacefully, "he'll not be looking at mantelshelf while he's poking the fire."

Oh, he'd some rum sayings had Tom Makepeace. Any road, I'd Dick Lacey's whistle in my pocket, so I slipped away while they were talking. I didn't think my father would miss me. In fact, he'd be glad to have me out of the way.

Well, it was only when I was scrambling down the river bank to get under the arch of Kingdom Bridge, that I began to wonder what the hell I was doing. Going to meet Dick Lacey! Going to meet the son of the man my father hated, and the lad that had dared our Daniel to his death! I couldn't work myself out.

I think now that that whistle was just an excuse. I *wanted* to go and meet him. I wanted his company. I was chasing after him like I'd chased our Dan. I was chasing after straws in the wind. I'd say I was that lonely and muddled, that this was what I was doing.

Any road, there was Kingdom Bridge, with its four great arches crossing the river, so I scrambled down the bank and found myself a seat on a bit of old driftwood. Aye, I'd be sitting there, waiting for Dick Lacey, with the handsome stone span soaring over my head. And gulls would fly under the arches, cackling, and looking down at you with their yellow eyes.

I'd a long wait. The tide was on the turn, and this was the tide that was meant to be bringing our horses. Water starts oozing up over the mud, and I'll tell you, it always gave me the strangest feeling to see the water in the river running upstream.

By that hour of the afternoon the sky was very dark and overcast, and I can remember that the air had a green look to it, like smoke. I was sitting there, looking across the river, looking at all the warehouses and steeples and mill chimneys and gantries in this queer storm light. And they looked exactly like they'd been etched in copper.

You know what it's like. It's a lonely business is waiting for someone. You begin to wonder if they're ever going to

59

come. And I'd be watching the fishing smacks being moved along the wall across the river. They'd be clearing the quayside for the steamboat coming in. The wind was splattering rain into my face, and you could taste the sea salt in it. And there'd be long swells of water slopping against the piers of the bridge and lumpy brown waves rearing midstream.

And I was sitting there thinking about Daniel, and I still think about him sometimes. I can remember how we used to play at wrestling. We'd stand back to back with our elbows locked, and I'd try to barrel-lift Dan by bending at the waist. Oh, I was missing my brother. And I think what I missed most was sharing a bed with him. I'd thump him for snoring down me neck, and he'd be complaining that my toe-nails were scratching his leg . . .

In the end, I took Dick Lacey's whistle out of my pocket, and there's only one thing you can do with a whistle when you've got it in your hand. And that's blow down it! So I did. I blew one sharp blast, and the men across the river would be shaking their fists at me. And that whistle blast stayed in my ears like deafness.

"That's mine," says Dick Lacey.

"Dick!" Well, I jumped up, glad to see him. But Dick Lacey stayed at the top of the bank, and he didn't come down.

"There must be something wrong with thee," he says.

I didn't glean what he meant, at first.

"Your Daniel's lying in the churchyard, and your father's after stretching me alongside. And there's you. What yer smiling for, Isaac Campion? Here, give us me whistle. Then I'm off."

Well, I climbed back up the bank to him, and gave him his whistle. What else could I do? What he'd said had given me a jolt, but I knew he was right.

"I still haven't told them it was you in the yard," I says.

"Why should I care? Tell your father. There's nowt he can do now."

60

The wind was knocking us about, and it was raining and all. Oh, it was a sad meeting. And it was our last meeting.

"I thought you said that you and Dan got on all right," I says.

"Aye. It didn't do us any good, did it? And you and me talking, that won't do any good," says Dick. And I can remember he rubbed his forehead with his hand, and says, "Oh, to hell with it all. I'm going away."

"Where to?"

"Richmond," he says. "I'm going to Richmond. I'll join a regiment there. They always need good men with horses. Oh, and I know all about horses. Me father's seen to that."

Now, this was an astonishing thought to me – that you could just up and go! I couldn't imagine it. "Does yer father know you're going?" I says.

"Oh aye! He knows. To hell with him. To hell with the lot of them. He's cut me out of his will. The business'll go to Margaret. Oh, she'll like that, will Margaret, and it'll put a smile on Bill Grafton's face and all. But I'm damned if I care."

Aye, his voice was bitter, but he'd made up his mind. And then he did a strange thing. I've never forgotten it, and I never shall. He took a gold sovereign out of his pocket and held it out to me.

"What's that fer?" I says.

"I owe your Daniel sixpence," he says. "The rest is luck-money."

Well, I didn't want it! I couldn't understand him. "I don't want that, Dick," I says.

"Take it!" He grabbed hold of my hand and wrapped my fingers round this coin. "Take it, yer stupid beggar. I don't care if you sling it in the river. But take it, damn yer!"

Then he walked away. And that was the last I saw of him, and that's how I remember him. In the rain. A tall lad of sixteen walking away from me, with his jacket flapping in the wind.

It was raining hard by then, and I stood looking down the river, over the salt marshes and out towards the estuary. I was a bit stunned, I suppose. And the sky was a mess of vicious green light and dirty clouds out over the sea. Well, I did what he'd said. I flung the gold sovereign as far as I could. I threw it into the river. And I expect it's still there.

Well, I have to confess it. As soon as I'd chucked that gold coin in the river, I began to regret it. It was a very great deal of money. And I began to think I should have kept it, and that I was a blamed fool. I'd thrown away twenty shillings – more money than I could have earned in two months as a day-boy to a farmer. And that seemed to prove to me that I was a fool. The sort of fool my father had always said I was. I'd cut my nose off to spite my face. I'd never get out of the stableyard. It was all useless and to hell with it. Dick Lacey was right, I thought.

And this was it. This was the heart of it. I was jealous of Dick Lacey because he was going to get away. He was walking out on all of it, and I felt more stuck than ever.

How can I explain it to you? Our stableyard was like a courtyard, with the old stable-block making the left wall of it, and the other stables across the back. Then the right side of the square was the wall of our house – kitchen and parlour. And the windows of both those rooms looked into the yard. And that was your world. That was my whole world. Eating and sleeping with horses. Shut in with them. Shut in my father's world, I was. And that was all my born days, and all the future I could see.

I stood there in the lashing rain, with nowhere else to go back to. And there was Dick Lacey marching away. And I was staring at the rough water in the river, and thinking about the boat that was due in.

Thinking of all those terrified mares slithering about in their own dung in the hold of that boat, out on the choppy sea.

And sometimes one of them would break a leg. It's not unknown. I'd seen it happen once, and I'd not care to see it again. The way that mare's knees were allowed to bang on the side of Harry Black's cart when he came to winch her out. And the way no one seemed bothered with her, because she was useless to them now, and was only a lump of live meat dangling in the winch-sling, and a waste of money.

Do you see what I'm trying to tell yer? Can you understand this world I was shut into? And why I'd had enough of it?

Ever since I was born, I'd seen all the indifferent cruelty that was inflicted on horses to make them work, or to trick a buyer into thinking a poor slow animal was frisky and spirited. And how patiently they bowed their heads to their lot, those working horses. I just knew that even if I tried all the days of my life I'd not stop feeling this awful pity for the lives and deaths of animals and men.

There's me, standing in the rain, watching a shoal of men and women flooding out of the gates of Glory Mill on the hill across the river. Spilling like black bees out of a basket onto the wet street. And off they'd scatter, hurrying home through that wind and rain, until they were all gone among the terraces and the streets.

I was rising thirteen, but that's what I was thinking as I walked home from the river. I was thinking, *I know I can endure it. I was put on the earth to endure it. But there must be more to living a life than this.*

Chapter Six

By the time I got in, Tom Makepeace and his stallion had gone. My father had changed out of his good clothes. He was sitting by the range, pulling on his boots. He was getting ready to go down to the quay to meet the boat, and he was arguing with my mother, about me.

"He's got to learn," he says. "You'd keep him tied to your apron, Alice. What good will that do him? He's got to learn."

"But you've got Harry and Dick-William. And the men on the boat," says my mother. I can remember her standing there by the range, holding the kettle. And she'd have a cloth wrapped round her hand, because the handles of those old iron kettles would get very hot. And on the table, there'd be three big tatie pies she'd made, ready for when these hired men came in. "What good can Isaac do at the boat?" she says.

My father doesn't answer. He stamps his foot into his boot.

But my mother won't have it. I was amazed at her. "Sam?" she says. "Samuel?" She was demanding an answer from him, and there's steam bulging and pluming from the spout of the kettle.

My Uncle Harry was there and all, but he had to keep out of it. He was standing by the door in a leather coat, waiting for my father. This was between my mother and father. He couldn't join in. So he's standing at the door, frowning out into the rain.

"He'll not melt," says my father.

"I know he won't. He's wet through already. You don't need him on the quay, Samuel. You don't need him. That's all I'm saying to yer. You've got all the men you need to bring the mares back. He'll just get in yer way."

"And he'll go on getting in the way until he learns summat!"

"He'd learn summat if you'd the patience to teach him!" My mother, raising her voice to him! I'd never heard of such a thing! I'd never heard her contradict him.

Aye. Masters and men. It makes you wonder why women ever stood for it. It makes you wonder how they put up with it. You'd think they'd have ganged up and banged their men's heads together. Well, that's what they're doing now. And it's not before time, I'd say.

But it was a wonder to hear my mother raise her voice to him then.

"You're too hard on him, Samuel," she says.

"No harder than I am on meself."

Uncle Harry's had enough of this. "Are we going or not? We've picked the right bloody night for it," he says.

"All right. All right. Have it your own way, woman," says my father. "But you mark my words, Alice. He's got to learn his place, and you're not helping him."

And off he tramps into the rain, with Uncle Harry shrugging his shoulders and following after him.

I think my mother must have been as surprised as me that she'd got her own way.

"Get your wet things off, Isaac," she says, and she'd be back at the range, making gravy for these tatie pies. Melting fat in a saucepan and stirring flour in. I can never hear the sound of a wooden spoon thumping softly on the bottom of a pan without thinking of her. And I can remember how the light used to shine up on her face when she'd open the fire-box door. That used to be one of my jobs – fetching in coal for her.

I sat down at the table, and I was thinking about the things that had happened that day. Thinking about my life and wondering what it all meant. And I felt a bit guilty that my mother had just fought this battle for me, but I was grateful as well.

"Don't peck at them pies," she says, and she's stirring her gravy. Well, I'd say there was a feeling between us. She'd just stood up to my father for me, and I felt I could say anything to her. I wanted to talk to her, and it was quiet in the kitchen. Our Becca must have been in bed.

"I don't believe what they tell you in church," I says.

"Yer what?"

"That the Lord's just. I don't believe it, Mam."

At any other time she'd have like as not clipped me round the ear for my blasphemy. But not that night.

"You're more like your father than you know," she says. And there'd be splats of gravy juice burning and sizzling on the hot-plate, frazzling away to black beads.

"I'll go to hell for saying things like that, won't I?" I says.

"That's what they tell you."

"Well, that proves it," I says. "You can't send someone to hell for saying what they think. That's not just. And you can't have folks grafting every hour God sends them, and then tell them they're an ignorant load o' sinners on Sunday. Half of them haven't got time to sin, have they? Do you think that's just, Mam?"

"Oh, Isaac Campion," she says. "Yer a deep swimming fish. Yer too deep for me."

Then I says, "Dick Lacey's gone away."

I thought she'd not heard for a moment. "Don't touch them pies," she says.

"I'm not doing."

"Dan was always a beggar for pecking at me pie crusts."

66

"Aye, I know," I says. "You thumped him on the head once with yer spoon."

"I'd forgotten that!" says me mother. And we were quiet for a bit.

"Where's Dick Lacey gone?" she says at last.

"Over Yorkshire way, he says. He's gone for a soldier."

Well, my mother turned round then and looked at me. "He *says*?"

I'd given myself away, so I had to tell her then. "Aye. I met him by Kingdom Bridge. He said his father'll cut him off without a penny, and Margaret'll get the business. And it sounds like that tramway's manager is courting her, you know."

"Isaac," my mother says. And she comes and sits at the table with me.

"Don't tell your father you talked to Dick Lacey. Don't tell him ever. I don't think I even want to know . . ."

"Aye, all right, Mam," I says.

"I'm glad Dick Lacey's gone," says my mother. "I'm glad he's got away."

Then she went and fetched a big blue and white striped jug out of the larder. She was going to go and fetch some beer for the men coming back.

But I took the jug off her. I wanted to do something for her, and there's a chasm of difference between *wanting* to do something for someone and *having* to do it.

"Take it down *The Turk's Head*, then," she says. "Ask Ma Eddishaw to fill it up. Tell her it's for Mrs Campion. She'll not mind."

And you could get a big jug of beer for fourpence in those days, and a bottle of malt whisky would cost you three and six.

My mother's gravy went cold, and the beer went flat in the jug, and we sat at that table together, waiting and waiting, until my mother's tatie pies were all hard and spoiled. The

67

rain went on raining, and the wind went on blowing. And still the mare and the men didn't come clattering into the yard.

I think that I knew something was up even before my mother did. I'd a suspicion of it. I'd seen the way that tide was coming in, and I'd seen the sky over the estuary.

I can remember a tale my mother used to tease me with. And I'm talking about when I was a very small boy now. She'd sit on the bed and she'd say:

"One dark and stormy night, three robbers sat in a cave, and the youngest robber said to his chieftain, 'Tell us a story.' And this is the story he told.

"'One dark and stormy night,' says the chieftain, 'three robbers sat in a cave, and the youngest robber says to his chieftain, Tell us a story.' And this is the story he told . . .'"

Well, it was like that, that night. Dark and stormy, and my mother and me waiting for my father to get back.

I'd started to get uneasy even before she set aside the shirt she was mending.

"Where can they be?" she says, and she went to the door. "Summat's happened, Isaac. I know it."

"They'll be in *The Crown and Anchor*," I says. "Perhaps they're leaving the mares on the boat until morning, when this wind has eased off." I didn't believe a word of it. Something was up.

"Your father'd not stop drinking," says my mother. "Your father'd have sent a lad to tell us if he were stopping drinking. Wouldn't he?"

"Not if he's arguing with the men over what he owes them. He always argues with Irish men if he owes them money," I says.

That made my mother laugh. It was true! Those Irish men were very good barterers. They'd not clap hands on a penny without a right good chin-wag. My father liked them for it, and I like them for it today.

"Aye, that's true!" says my mother. "That's true enough."

So we sat, and we sat, and we sat.

"Perhaps a mare's bolted in town. Happen they're rounding her up," says my mother, and she starts clicking a fingernail between her teeth.

I said I would go out and see what was happening, but my mother wouldn't have it.

"Oh no," she says. "No, yer don't. I'm not sitting here fretting about you and all. I'm not losing me cavalry because I've lost me scouts."

And that's how it went on. Every time we heard a cart go past the gate, or footsteps in the street, my mother would go to the door. "Is it them?"

But it was nearly midnight before my Uncle Harry turned up. And neither my father was with him and nor were the Irish mares.

"What is it? What's to do?" cries my mother, when Uncle Harry comes staggering in with rain tipping off the brim of his hat.

"What's happened, Harry?"

"The boat's not come in," he says. "They say it set off from the Isle o' Man, but it's not come in. And now the bloody tide's gone out." His words were slithering and slurring off his tongue, and he was swaying against the door-post.

"Where's me father, Uncle Harry?" I says.

"Int' *Crown and Anchor* stables. I made him doss down in the straw. Don't worry, Alice. He's just had a drop too much. Ah, God Almighty, so have I. Let me sit down afore me pins give way."

"He's drunk?" my mother says. "You left Samuel in the stables *drunk*!"

"Aye," says Uncle Harry. "Don't fuss. Ah, Lord help us, I'd forgotten what a beggar for the beer he gets after he's poured the first two down his neck."

Well, my mother grabbed her shawl off the door. "You

left him *drunk*?" But Uncle Harry put out his hand and caught her by the arm. "Alice! Yer not going out. He's all right where he is."

"Don't you tell me what to do in my own house, Harold Campion!" I thought she was going to wallop him! Instead, she sat down again, still clutching her shawl in her hands.

"You could have sent someone to tell us, Harry," she says.

"Aye, I suppose I could . . . When the boat didn't turn up, me and Sam walked down the river to the light. It's blowing a bloody gale out off the sandbank. We went back to the *Crown* for a livener to warm oursel's up."

Well, Uncle Harry's rubbing his eyes and shaking his head. And I'm just watching him.

"I'd forgotten what a beggar he is for the beer."

"And you got drunk."

"And we got drunk, Alice. There was nowt else to do. Eh, he's a bad beggar when he's had a skinful. I thought he'd left off that game when the old man died . . ."

"He did," says my mother. "Oh Harry . . ."

Then Uncle Harry grabs hold of me. And his breath stank of beer and cigars. And what he said pierced right through me. "I'm telling yer, lad," he says. "It's a bad do when yer glad to see the back of your own father. And me and Sam were glad to see the back of that old devil, I'll tell yer! Yer grandfather. He was as sober as a stone and as cold as charity was *Mister* Reuben Campion. You don't remember your grandfather, do yer, lad?"

I shook my head at him.

"That's enough, Harry," says me mother. "Yer drunk."

"I know, lass. I know. I can't tell you a lie." Uncle Harry bursts out laughing. "I'm damned if I can even stand up! How the devil I got home, I don't know. Stop gawping at me, lad."

I was gawping at him. I was staring at him and he was breaking my heart, so to speak. I'd been making a bit of a hero out of Uncle Harry, and now here he was, wrenching bits off the crust of my mother's tatie pies. The crumbs were spilling down his chin, and they were sticking to his coat. And his eyes looked as if they were swimming off in two different directions.

And this was my Uncle Harry, with his smooth hands, and his neatly trimmed moustache, and his cigars that smelled of faraway cities . . .

I burned with embarrassment to see him like that. To see him with pie crumbs spattering his chin and his chest.

Any road, my mother whispers to me to get away to my bed. And I was glad to go. I was glad to get out of the kitchen, for I'd seen a new light on my hero. I'd seen his feet of human clay.

I must have got some sleep that night, because I can remember being woken in the dark. Something had woken me up just before dawn. At first I thought it must have been little Becca coughing. She'd be asleep with her head against my arm.

Well, I lay awake for a long while in that blind light, waiting for the day to dawn. And I was thinking about the boat. Grieving for it. In my mind's eye I could see it foundering in the lurching waves. The cold salt sea crashing through the hatches and pouring down on the terrified mares in the hold. How they'd plunge and rear in the dark, as the water crashed in on them . . .

Perhaps the boat hadn't set off, but, no, Uncle Harry had said that it had. Perhaps it had been blown down the coast, or had run for shelter to some other harbour.

I lay there, not wanting to face our bad luck. It seemed to me that we'd had more than our share, and there was no sense in the world.

The Irish have a song, and they are some of the finest singers in the land.

"When misfortune falls,
Sure, no man can shun it."

71

That is the song they sing, but it is a hard thing for a boy to believe.

And I was thinking about my father, and what would become of us all. It was the pattern of all our lives my mind was running on, and it still runs on it today.

It seemed to me there was a pattern in what my Uncle Harry had said about my grandfather, and about my father and him being glad to see the back of their own flesh and bone.

I can remember watching my father, the winter before Dan died. Watching him carving a toy for our Becca in a few cold nights of the year. This had stayed in my mind, because I'd seen something new in him. And I can still see the way that wood curled like wax away from the blade of his knife. It didn't splinter or fray the way it would have done if I'd tried to carve it.

Had me father wanted to be a dealer like his father? There he'd sat by the range whittling out the tiny ears and nostrils of this toy horse for Becca, and it ran on little wooden wheels. I can remember his long calm concentrated gaze as he sat there carving it by the range, blowing the wood-shavings into the coal-hod. He could have been a craftsman with wood, I'd say, if he'd been apprenticed to a cabinet-maker.

There I lay, watching the sky turn grey and the dawn come on. And I was wondering why it should be that you were born and didn't have any choice. And I'd be thinking perhaps if you were rich you had choices. Perhaps if you were born rich you didn't have to follow in your father's footsteps to the end of your life.

Oh, it was a right cat's-cradle of notions I was weaving in me head. Thinking what it would be like to be a rich man's son.

I remember once, when I was seven or eight, a handsome trap stopped outside our yard. A gentleman had come to see my father about something, but I don't remember what. A rich man, in an astrakhan coat, with a collar of lamb's wool.

72

Me and Daniel had been ratting in the old stable, and we'd just come out with Dick-William's terrier dancing about Dan's feet, and he'd be carrying a couple of brown rats by their tails. Well, we got a surprise. There was a boy standing by the gate. The son of this gentleman, in tailored clothes. A very blond, clean-looking boy. But he was gazing at Dan's dead rats with a look of pure bloody longing on his face! He wanted to come over and talk to us, and I reckon he would have swopped the coat off his back for one o' them dead tailies.

But his father called him away. He had no choice. He'd to do as his father tells him. "Coming, Papa," he says. And that boy would grow into a gentleman, and I expect that never once in his whole living life, did he go ratting in a barn.

Well, that was the way of things, I supposed. They had to be endured. Only here was Dick Lacey walking out of his father's yard! But I'd no mind to become a soldier. I'd had enough of obeying orders to last me the rest of me days!

In the end I got up from my bed. I couldn't get back to sleep, and there was no point lying there. Besides, I could hear someone moving about downstairs. I thought it was my Uncle Harry. So I got up and pulled on my clothes, and went down into the hallway.

There's thumps and shuffles coming from behind our kitchen door, and a few groans. It made me a bit nervous to go in.

It was getting on for dawn by now, and it'd be dim and misty in our hallway. Even in daytime it was quite a dim place, because the front door was hardly ever opened. We didn't have many what you would call front-door visitors.

Well, there's me standing on the cold tiles, clutching me boots. And that wind of the night before had dropped away. It was still and silent. The storm had blown itself out, and the day was dawning clear.

I'll tell you something else about our hallway. Something I've never forgotten. On the wall was the stuffed head of my

73

grandfather Reuben's favourite dog. When it had died, he'd had its head mounted. It used to stare at you with its glass eyes, like a fish. And under it was a brass plaque.

> *'Here is a Pattern for the Human Race,*
> *A Dog that did His Work and Knew his Place.'*

I never did get used to seeing it, and whenever you walked through our hallway, its glass eyes followed you, like the eye of God!

Any road, this groaning and bumping's going on in the kitchen, and I thought it was my Uncle Harry suffering from the demon drink. So I pushed open the door. But it wasn't me Uncle Harry.

I'll tell you what I saw.

I saw an old, old man slumped forward on a chair, with his elbows on his knees and his head in his hands. And there were bits of straw stuck in his coat and in his hair. And on the floor next to him was a broken cup.

I expect it must have been the sound of that cup breaking which had woken me, and my father had cut his hand on it. Aye, that's who it was, slumped in his chair. It was me father.

And I'll tell you, I would rather have heard him shouting than have seen him like that, groaning like a sheep with his head in his hands.

Well, I crept back out of the kitchen, still clutching my boots in my hand. My father hadn't seen me. And I went and sat on the bottom step of the stairs.

I wished I'd never got up from my bed. I'd sooner have had me father knock me down again, than seen him like that. How can I explain it to yer?

For all that I'd been thinking about him. For all the notions I had. Outside the stableyard gates, across the river, was a world of workhouses, and of thundering black cotton mills where thin lads of my own age, but half my height, had to creep between machines. There was the black County

Asylum on the hill, where Joe Flitch's brothers were locked up. There were magistrates and assizes, and the poisonous smoke that belched out of Phoenix foundry, and there were cramped terraces of spitting, coughing thin men.

Me father's hand was hard. It could come whistling out of nowhere, but he stood between that world and me.

And now here he was, coughing and moaning like a sheep, and that world loomed up over our yard like a shadow.

There's me, huddled on the stairs, and the first jackdaws are flying over the chimneys, and the first gulls are mewing and cackling over the river. One look at my father had convinced me that the boat had gone down. Even now, the first drowned horses would be washing to and fro in the grey surf of the shallows out beyond the salt-marshes, with their manes and tails floating like seaweed. The poor, beautiful drowned horses, that had less choice than men. That had been herded into the stinking hold of the boat to be brought to the town, to be set between cart-shafts.

Oh, the patient, placid horses, that dragged the whole weight of work behind them, and endured the halters, the collars, the bits, the bridles, the blinkers and whips of kind masters and of cruel, until they were done for, and sent to the knacker's, or buried in a ditch.

I put me head in my hands, and I wept for them, and for all the drowned horses washed to the shore.

Chapter Seven

I DON'T KNOW HOW LONG my father had been standing in the kitchen doorway watching me. "Get yersel' to the pump," he says. And by this he meant the pump out in our yard. He was holding onto the door frame. He wasn't steady on his feet.

"You've cut yer hand," I says.

"Aye. Gawp yer fill, lad. Tha's not seen me afore like this."

I went out into the yard with him. He had his hand on my shoulder, to steady himself. It was as heavy as a stone.

The storm had washed the sky clear. And this is how it happens with those spring storms. One minute they're raging and the next it is the sweetest day.

Well, my father props himself up on the grey helmet of the pump, and I'd to work the handle. Up and down. Up and down. And he was wincing at the racket it made. The pump would be spitting and belching, but you could tell when the water was rising, because the handle got heavier and firmer in your hand, and then the water would gush out.

My father pulls off his coat that's all filthy with straw, and he pulls his shirt off over his head, and then he shoves his face and his neck into the stream of cold water. By Christ, it was cold! But he stayed there for a long minute, with that icy water streaming through his hair.

Then he comes up shuddering, and shaking the water from his face.

"Me shirt!"

I gave it to him, and he towelled himself dry with it, then he chucks it from him, and puts his dirty coat back on. He slipped it on over his bare shoulders, and he looked like a tramp.

"The devil," he says. "I could do wi' a jug of beer to drink mesel' sober . . ."

I went and fetched that jug of flat beer for him that was in the kitchen. He gulped it down in great gulps, then he wipes his mouth on his sleeve.

"Well, you've seen the lot now," he says to me. "You've seen the bloody lot."

I wanted to say something about the boat and the horses. But I couldn't. I could not find words. "Uncle Harry says you dossed down int' *Crown and Anchor* stables," I says at last.

"Yer Uncle Harry's a damn liar," says my father. "He locked me in the stables, and it's taken me all night to get out."

"Locked you in! Why?"

Well, my father sits down on the cobbles by the pump, and he looked more like a tramp than ever, with that empty beer jug dangling between his knees. "Never you mind," he says. "No, I'll tell yer. I'll tell yer why. Your mother says I've to teach you summat, so I'll teach yer summat now! Steamboat didn't arrive last night."

"I know," I says. I wanted to comfort him, you see. At that moment, I thought the state he was in was all due to this misfortune.

"And if it doesn't turn up, we've got two pregnant mares and a gelding between us and workhouse, by my reckoning," he says.

I tried to tell him that we'd manage. That we'd get by, but, do you know, he wasn't taking a blind bit of notice of me. Perhaps it was the fumes of that beer gone straight back to his head, because he wasn't really talking to me, he was talking down into that empty jug. And his words were running on that same old bitter road. On that treadmill. Even in the middle of all this, that was happening, he was obsessed with it.

"But that wasn't enough," he's saying. "No, there had to be more . . . He sticks to me like tar, that devil. Whatever I touch he cocks his leg at. Them horses I sold to tramways were masterpieces. And now that devil's got his hands on them. I *knew* summat was up! I knew it all along. There's summat up between Bill Grafton and Clem Lacey, I told Jack. And I was right.

"Bill Grafton buys masterpieces of horses, and electrifies the tramways. And all the while he's courting Margaret bloody Lacey!"

I couldn't understand him. I stood there looking down at him, where he was sat on the dirty cobbles. And I couldn't understand him. And I still can't. It was an obsession. It was an unholy hatred. It mattered more to him, by then, than anything else in the world.

"How can Clem Lacey get his hands on them horses?" I says. I couldn't understand why it mattered. Me father had been paid for them by the tramways. So what the hell did it matter?

"I'll tell yer how he gets his hands on them! Bill Grafton gets wind o' this electrification business, and ups and buys those marvels off me. Then he sells them to his new father-in-law dirt cheap! And that devil's got them in his stables now."

Well, his coat is open on his bare chest, and he slowly looks round our empty yard. There's only the gelding with the bandaged foot looking over the stable door. And all the rest are empty. The Clydesdale mare was back in Crook's field, and the piebald mare was out in the paddock.

He looks along the empty row of stable doors, and says, "The cold light o' day, eh . . . If yer put yer hands in a fire, they'll get burned . . . I knew I was putting me hands in the fire wi' that deal, but I didn't know which way the smoke was blowing. No, I didn't know that."

"But why did Uncle Harry lock you up?" I says.

"Because if I could have laid me hands on me gun last night, I'd have blown Clem Lacey to Kingdom Come in bits. And I might just do it yet."

I didn't want to hear any more of it. I couldn't understand why his mind was running on this track when we were in this mess. All I could think of was the workhouse on the hill, and the drowned horses under the sea.

So I left him and went back inside.

He went on sitting there all morning. I can still see him. A black lump, like a vagrant, keeping company with the water pump. My mother didn't come downstairs for a long time. And I suppose this was her way of reproaching him for his drunkenness and for the state he was in.

I couldn't think what to do, apart from brew up a kettle of black tea for him. So that's what I did.

Then my Uncle Harry poked his head round the kitchen door. "Isaac?"

"He's back," I says.

"What's he saying?" Uncle Harry looked almost as wrecked as my father.

"Says you locked him int' stable to stop him shooting Clem Lacey."

"He's not still on after that! Pass us a drop of that tea, Isaac."

So I gave him a cup.

"What did he say about me?"

"Nowt," I says. "He called you a damn liar, that's all."

"All! Ah well, I'll stay in here until he sobers up."

Well, I asked him if he thought me father really would shoot Clem Lacey, but Uncle Harry shook his head.

"No," he says. "It's all talk. And even if he wanted to, I've had a tinker wi' his gun."

Uncle Harry came and sat at the kitchen table with me for a time, and he must have drunk damn near a gallon of black tea. I kept brewing up for him.

"Uncle Harry," I says. "I keep thinking about those poor horses on that boat, and the men."

"Aye well," says Uncle Harry, "I sometimes think we bring our own bad luck on our heads."

"Yer mean it's our fault? Our fault that a boat goes down!" I couldn't believe it. No, no, no. I wasn't having that!

"No," says Uncle Harry, "that's not what I mean. But you can make sure your cargo's insured for a start! That's what you can do, lad. But, Sam, he's just like yer grand-father. He thinks it's all clap hands on a deal, hide a bad hoof wi' blacking and a nettle up its tail to mek it dance!"

I could see he was right. I'd no answer to that. There's me sitting with me chin in me hands, wondering what's to become of us all.

Then Uncle Harry says, "Listen, Isaac. You know I'm going to America at the end of the summer, don't yer?"

"Aye."

"Well, I want you to come with me. I don't know what it'll be like when we get there, but that's one good reason for going, lad. To see summat new!"

It was like being given treasure, and then seeing it snatched away again.

"How can I?" I says. "I can't leave me mother with all this."

Uncle Harry didn't try and persuade me, he just shrugged, and then he went into the parlour, to sleep off his bad head.

When my mother came down at last, my father was still sitting in the yard. "And he can stay there till Judgement

Day!" says me mother. "He can stay there until the Trumpet sounds!"

We were all waiting for me father to move, you see. Waiting for him to do something. His sitting was like a punishment and a curse on all our heads.

"Why doesn't he get across to the shipping-office?" says me mother. "To see what the news is? Him sitting there like a tramp. That's not going to help. What if a buyer comes for that gelding and cab? And him sitting there like a tramp."

In the end she turned to me. "Isaac, you go. Not across the quay. They'd like as not kick a lad from the office. Get yersel' up Harrow Hill and see what yer can."

I didn't think there was any point, but I couldn't tell her that. All the horses and drovers, passengers and sailors were just floating wreckage on the sea. Well, I couldn't tell her that. And anything was better than just waiting for me father to move. It was a relief to run out of our gateway, and I wished I could run all the way to America and never come back.

Oh, it seemed a bitter thing to me, that the sun should be shining in a clear blue sky. And that the whole bloody world seemed to be full of blackbirds singing and hawthorn blossoming, when I'd this sorrow inside me. I couldn't make sense of any of it, and, I'll tell you, I ran up Harrow Lane. Ran until my chest was bursting, to try and shut all this out.

I wanted to go with Uncle Harry more than anything. But I just couldn't see my way to it. I kept thinking, if only he'd asked me before this happened. If only he'd have asked me yesterday.

Can you see? I felt it was my duty but it was a duty I didn't want. I felt I'd to stay, to help me father get his business back on its feet. And here I was, not even wanting to inherit that business. And yet I thought I should stay. For the sake of my mother, and for our Becca, and the baby.

Oh, I didn't expect that my father would change. He'd go on making a stick out of the Laceys to beat his own back.

Aye, I ran up Harrow Hill, until I'd a pain in my chest. And then I'd to slow down and catch my breath.

Daniel was dead. And Dick Lacey had gone for a soldier, and here was the one chance in my life to get away.

Well, I got to the gate of Crook's field, and I climbed up onto it and sat there, looking down at the river shining in all that sunlight, but I knew what I'd see. The river was low again, and there was only one fishing smack still moored against the quay.

So I sat, like my father, staring down at the black chimneys of the town against all that blue sky, knowing that the best thing I could do for my own life would be to go, and knowing I had to stay.

Well, my eyes must have got a bit blurred with staring down at the river. It's very intense, is that bright sunlight on water. It half blinds you. I know I wasn't weeping. I was beyond tears by then.

Any road, I rubs my eyes, and there's a flight of pigeons swerving off over the roof tops. I've never forgotten them. Whenever I see pigeons, I think of this day. I watched them swerve off together, and it's a marvel is the way those birds fly. They turn together in the air like a single thought, and I watched them as they headed off down the river and down over the marshes. I kept them in sight as far as I could, and I suppose I was straining after them, out over the sea.

Then, "No!" I turned right round on the gate, jammed the toes of my boots between the bars, and stood up on the second rung.

It was off the sandbank, in the channel, waiting for the tide to rise again so that it could come up river to Kingdom Quay! As small as a child's toy, the grey and white steamboat! Riding safe at anchor on that shining estuary!

It was as if all the drowned horses had come alive again, and were galloping up out of the sea! I was shouting and waving my hand, but no one could have seen us from the boat. I was up on Harrow Hill, far away.

Well, I didn't run home. No, I walked quietly down Harrow Hill. I took that steamboat as my sign, and I knew by the time I turned in through the gateway of our stable-yard, that once the Irish mares were sold, I'd tell my father I was leaving. And, by the end of the summer, I'd be gone.

November 2nd 1984

Dear Miss Howker,

Thank you for coming to see me. I will tell you it did me a power of good. All those folks are dead now, even our Becca who was 72 when she passed away. I went to America with Uncle Harry like I told you as I could not live in that house with my father any longer. But I came back to Hardacre in 1913 when he died. I'm sorry to say it was from drinking it killed him, and the business was in a mess. Of course the war came on and I joined up. I got out of that in one piece. Dick Lacey was blown to Kingdom Come on the Somme. It was a bit of hard luck for him, and I was very sorry to hear it.

There was no future in horses after so I hired myself out to a farmer and learned to plough with a team, then with a tractor after Hitler's war come on. It was not all a bed of roses but I don't complain.

One thing else I wanted to tell you. I have a notion in my head that children weren't invented until after the Great War. In that time of day when I was born, you weren't children with toys like they are these days. You were just a damn nuisance and a mouth to feed until you could do a day's work.

Come and see me again soon but it will have to be soon or I'll be gone. I like this notion of reincarnation which I was reading about in the paper. I hope I come back as a bird next time, a swift or a swallow. It seems to me they have a damn good time flying about and are without cares.

*I remain
    your obedient servant,
    Isaac Campion*

ISAAC
CAMPION
1888-1984